Aidan Chambers' Book of
GHOSTS AND HAUNTINGS

Dim and ghostly figures walking through walls; strange and unexplained cries and wails; things that go bump in the night – these are all the classic components of hauntings. Ghosts are fascinating, but they are also frightening and it is reassuring to know that it is now possible to make a more scientific classification of different types of ghosts. They fall into four distinct groups: experimental ghosts, crisis ghosts, post-mortem ghosts and ghosts who persistently haunt the same place.

In this book Aidan Chambers has gathered together a fascinating collection of material relating to each ghost type, illustrated with some remarkable pictures. He has drawn extensively on the papers of the Society for Psychical Research. The Society has an extremely factual and objective approach in its research into all things spiritualistic and ghostly and Renée Haynes, a member of the Society's council, suggests ways of setting about a ghost hunt.

There are also sections on spiritualism, the problems of photographing ghosts, mediums and séances, poltergeists, and a brief guide to some of the more interesting haunted houses of Great Britain and Ireland.

Aidan Chambers' Book of

Ghosts and Hauntings

Puffin Books

Puffin Books, Penguin Books Ltd,
Harmondsworth, Middlesex, England
Penguin Books, 625 Madison Avenue,
New York, New York 10022, U.S.A.
Penguin Books Australia Ltd,
Ringwood, Victoria, Australia
Penguin Books Canada Ltd, 2801 John Street,
Markham, Ontario, Canada L3R 1B4
Penguin Books (N.Z.) Ltd, 182–190 Wairau Road,
Auckland 10, New Zealand

First published simultaneously by Puffin Books
and Longman Young Books 1973
Reprinted in Puffin Books 1979

This anthology copyright © Aidan Chambers, 1973
Illustrations © Penguin Books Ltd, 1973
All rights reserved

Made and printed in Great Britain by
Richard Clay (The Chaucer Press) Ltd,
Bungay, Suffolk
Set in Intertype Lectura

Except in the United States of America, this book
is sold subject to the condition that it shall not,
by way of trade or otherwise, be lent, re-sold,
hired out, or otherwise circulated without the
publisher's prior consent in any form of binding
or cover other than that in which it is published and
without a similar condition including this condition
being imposed on the subsequent purchaser

For William and Ellen Tucker

Contents

Illustrations

Acknowledgements

I am particularly indebted to the Society for Psychical Research for permission to quote at length from their records and, in acknowledging the following sources, acknowledge at the same time my gratitude: Crisis ghost Bowyer-Bower, p. 42, *Proceedings*, XXXIII, p. 170; crisis ghost M'Connel, p. 43, S.P.R. records quoted in *Apparitions and Haunted Houses* by Sir Ernest Bennett (Faber and Faber, 1939); post-mortem ghost Mrs P, p. 48, *Proceedings*, VI, p. 26; ghost, p. 52, *Proceedings*, III, p. 102; 'Miss Morton', a slightly shortened version, p. 57, *Proceedings*, VIII, p. 311; Swanland poltergeist, p. 98, *Proceedings*, VII; Enniscorthy poltergeist, p. 117, *Proceedings*, XXV.

The sources of other quotations in this book are acknowledged as follows: *The Haunted Homes and Family Traditions of Great Britain* by John H. Ingram (Reeves & Turner, 1905). This adapted version first appeared in *Haunted Houses* by Aidan Chambers (Pan-Piccolo). *More Tales from the Fens* by W. H. Barrett (Routledge & Kegan Paul, 1964). *Legends of Devon* by J. R. W. Coxhead (Western Press, 1954). *In My Solitary Life* by Augustus Hare (1871). *Phantasms of the Living* by E. Gurney, F. W. H. Myers, and R. Podmore (Trubner & Co., 1886). *Psychical Research Today* by D. J. West (Duckworth, 1954). *English Fairy Tales* by Joseph Jacobs (Bodley Head, 1968). *'Spirit' Photography* by Simeon Edmunds (S.P.R., 1965).

PART ONE

Ghosts go haunting . . .

1 · The Place is Haunted!

Hardly a week goes by without a ghost getting into the news. Just as I was about to start writing this book a sober and serious newspaper, the *Daily Telegraph*, published the following item:

WEST POINT
The ghost of a cavalryman of about 140 years ago is causing such a furore at the United States Military Academy at West Point, that the room it haunts is being closed until spring. Normally two first-year cadets sleep in the room.

At about the same time, other newspapers were telling their readers of a sailor who claimed he had taken a photograph of a ghost while it haunted his ship.

Stories like these are the tip of a very large spectral iceberg. They are the ghosts we all hear about because they attract publicity. But for every one that gets into the news there are scores that do not. Some hauntings become world famous – the Drummer of Tedworth, the ghost of Hinton Ampner, the phenomena of Calvados Castle, the poltergeist of Epworth Parsonage – and are argued about endlessly. Others are humbler narratives, no more than local or family legends, handed down from old to young, generation after generation, each teller of the story changing a bit here and adding a dramatic touch there, until, in the end, the tale bears little resemblance to the original event.

Sorting out the fact from the fiction in ghost stories is the first, most difficult task for serious students of PSYCHICAL PHENOMENA. What, for example, are we to make of the ghost

15

of Lady Hoby? Her spectral figure used to appear – and still does for all I know – at Bisham Abbey House, a fourteenth-century building now used as a physical training centre. (Perhaps the constant companionship of tireless gymnasts will wear the old ghost out and frighten it away.) The story goes that during the reign of Henry VIII's daughter, Queen Mary, her half-sister, Princess Elizabeth, was kept prisoner at Bisham in the custody of Sir Thomas Hoby. The princess must have liked her gaoler, because when she became queen she appointed him to the important post of Ambassador to France.

Lady Hoby, Sir Thomas's wife, died in the abbey house in 1609, and since then many people claim to have seen her ghost. They recognize the apparition because it looks like Lady Hoby's portrait, which hangs in the abbey hall. Though there is one curious difference: the spirit always is like the 'negative' of a photograph, the dark parts showing light and the light parts dark. It is usually seen gliding out of a bedroom with a basin of water floating along in front of it in which the ghost washes its blood-stained hands.

A sad story is told about this restless phantom. Lady Hoby was very clever, a scholar who knew Greek and Latin and wrote poetry. But she had a son called William who was so dull-witted, so slow at learning, and so untidy, constantly making blots on his copy-books, that he frequently angered his mother, who would punish him brutally. One day, Lady Hoby thrashed poor William so badly the boy died. Not long afterwards, no doubt from remorse and guilt (or so the story would have us believe), Lady Hoby died also.

What evidence is there to support this gruesome tale? Very little, in fact, and that not at all convincing. In 1840 some workmen are supposed to have found, stuffed behind a skirting board, a few ink-stained copy-books bearing William Hoby's name. Unfortunately these vital clues seem to have been lost soon after they were brought to light – a curious mischance considering that apart from the copy-books no other trace of the existence of the unhappy boy has ever been found. Lady Hoby, we know for certain, had five children, four by her first marriage and one by her second. But none of them was called William.

Whatever the truth of the matter, the Bisham ghost can unsettle the sanest of men. At one time the abbey was owned by an Admiral Vansittart. He describes how one night he had been playing chess with his brother in the room where the Lady Hoby's portrait hangs. 'We had finished playing,' he wrote, 'and my brother had gone up to bed. I stood for some time with my back to the wall, turning the day over in my mind. Minutes passed. I looked round. It was Dame Hoby. The frame on the wall was empty! Terrified, I fled from the room.' If salty old admirals are not safe from such terrors, what hope have the rest of us? Though, I must admit, to my mind ghosts that materialize from painted pictures, leaving the canvas bare, are more at home in comic horror films than in real life and I find myself wondering whether the admiral had not taken one glass of rum too many.

PSYCHICAL PHENOMENA

Anything which is psychical *has to do not with the solid material world but with the mind or the soul. Thus, apparitions are psychical phenomena because they exist in our minds and do not have solid, physical form, even though we think we see them standing in front of us like ordinary living people. Visions, dreams, nightmares, and such-like are all psychical: they belong to our inner lives, though they may be telling us about our outer lives in the physical 'natural' world.*

Ghosts go haunting . . .

The stately homes of Britain teem with such spectres, more heard about in spooky yarns than come across in reality. Some are wild and probably fictional from beginning to end, like the wraith of Earl Petrie said to gamble with the Devil in Glamis Castle. Others are spine-chilling, fearful to look upon, and may have some basis in fact, like the eyeless Brown Lady of Raynham Hall, Norfolk — a spectre that was once shot at by a famous author and photographed by a less nervous victim of her appearances. Still others are kindly, or amusing, or melancholy, or never materialize at all but cause unsettling noises just at the time you least expect them. Most, it should be added, are harmless, minding their own ethereal business so long as everybody else minds his. My favourite of all, because it has an interesting history and concerns a lovely house, is the ghost of Burton Agnes Hall, near Driffield, Yorkshire.

OWD NANCE OF BURTON AGNES

Burton Agnes Hall, a beautiful Tudor mansion, was built by Anne Griffith with money left by her wealthy father to her two sisters and herself. Lively, energetic, much loved, Anne was attacked by robbers while out walking and mortally wounded shortly after the Hall was finished. In the last moments of her life she asked her sisters to promise that, after her death, they would remove her head from her body and keep it in the house she had worked so hard to create. To please Anne, the distressed sisters agreed, but after her death they could not bring themselves to carry out such a gruesome promise.

The funeral was three days over when, during the night, such a dreadful crash was heard that the sisters and servants alike were terrified. Nothing could be found that might account for the row, however: all was safe and secure in its place. A week later – on the same night of the week that Anne died – a series of appalling noises broke out, waking the entire household: heavy, stamping footsteps running along passages, followed by the crash of violently closed doors. Again, though the house was searched from top to bottom, no explanation could be discovered and nothing at all was damaged. Another week, and the noises came again, with increased vehemence and accompanied this time by agonized, deathly screams.

Next morning the servants left, unable to bear the haunting any longer, and the two confused sisters called in the vicar for help. When he heard what had happened, he persuaded the sisters to exhume Anne's corpse and carry out their promise. So the coffin was raised and opened. All was in order, just as it had been three weeks before. Except for one shocking detail. Anne's head was no longer attached to her body. More astonishing still, the flesh and hair had disappeared, leaving a white and grinning skull.

Anne, always called Owd Nance by the local people, was a determined woman during her lifetime, and even from her grave managed to get her way. The skull was taken into the house, and has remained there till this day. Sometimes, a rash new owner tries to rid the place of its heirloom, but always the ghastly haunting ensures that the skull is brought back at once. Now it rests secure behind a carved screen, safe from meddling hands. And Anne, dressed in black and with her sisters beside her, looks down on curious visitors from a portait that hangs on a wall.

Many legends surround the skull, most of them old wives' tales without a grain of truth in them. But one story I especially enjoy. It was told to his cousin by a Mr John Bilton the day after the night described, and found its way into print when Mr J. H. Ingram included it in his book, *The Haunted Homes and Family Traditions of Great Britain*. John Bilton had a strong nerve and did not believe in ghosts, but he told his cousin that he had never passed such a frightening night in his life before and that he would never again sleep at the Hall no matter how large a prize he was offered for doing so. This is his cousin's account of the incident:

Some forty years ago, John Bilton, a cousin of mine, came from London on a visit to the neighbourhood of Burton Agnes Hall, and, having a relative, Matthew Potter, who was game-keeper on the estate and resided at the Hall, he paid him a visit, and was invited to pass the night there. Potter, however, told John that, according to popular report, the house was haunted, and that if he was afraid of ghosts he had better sleep elsewhere. But John, who was a dare-devil sort of fellow, replied,

'Afraid! Not I indeed. I care not how many ghosts there may be in the house so long as they do not molest me.'

Potter then told him of the skull and of the painted portrait of Owd Nance that hung in one of the rooms, and asked if he would like to see the picture. John replied that he would, and they went into the room where it was hanging. Potter held a light before the portrait, when, in a moment and without apparent cause, the light went out and defied all attempts to rekindle it. Matthew and John were obliged to grope their way to their bedroom in the dark.

They had to sleep in the same bed, and Matthew was soon asleep and snoring. But John, thinking of the tale of the skull and the curious circumstances of the sudden extinguishing of the light in front of the picture, lay awake. He had been thinking about an hour, when he heard a shuffling of feet outside the bedroom door, which at first he ascribed to the servants going to bed. But as the sounds did not cease, but kept increasing, he nudged Matthew and said,

'Matty, what the devil is all that row about?'

'Jinny Yewlats [owls],' replied Potter in a half-waking tone, and turning over, again began to snore.

The noises became more frantic, and it seemed ten or a dozen persons were shuffling about in the passage just outside, and rushing in and out of rooms, slamming doors with great violence, upon which John gave his friend another vigorous nudge in the ribs, ex-claiming,

'Wake up, Matty. Don't you hear that confounded row? What does it mean?'

'Jinny Yewlats,' again muttered his companion.

'Jinny Yewlats!' replied John Bilton. 'Jinny Yewlats can't make such an infernal uproar as that!'

Matty, who was now awake, listened a moment, and then said, 'It's Owd Nance, but I never take any notice of her.' And he rolled over again and began to snore.

After this the fun began fast and furious! A struggling fight seemed to be going on outside, and the clapping of doors reverberated in the passage like thunderclaps. John expected every moment to see the door fly open and Owd Nance with a troop of ghosts come rushing in. But no such catastrophe occurred, and after a while the noises ceased, and about daybreak John fell asleep.

Burton Agnes is not the only place possessed of a skull said to cause trouble if anyone tries to remove it from its resting place. The more interesting of the others are: Bettiscombe Manor, Dorset; the Abbey at Bury St Edmunds, Suffolk; Calgarth Hall, Westmorland; and Wardley Hall, Lancashire.

It would be a mistake, however, to think that ghosts haunt only old and grand houses. In the documented records of the Society for Psychical Research (see page 139) as well as among the local legends that abound everywhere in Britain, are many accounts of disturbances in quite ordinary places: in council flats and factories, in hotels and country cottages, in schools and offices, on busy streets where no one expects to find ghosts and on dark and lonely moorland pathways where everyone expects to find them. Ghosts go haunting anywhere and everywhere, by day or night, and at any season of the year.

The problem for the serious student is to sort out the credible from the incredible, the fact from the fiction. Where does he start? Renée Haynes gives some answers to that question in Chapter 12. He begins, she suggests, at home, collecting all the reports, ancient and modern, of the ghosts said to haunt his neighbourhood. And these he sifts, attempting to sort out the details and to judge their worth as evidence. This needs some knowledge and guidance if you haven't done anything like it before. Help of this kind can be got from books, a list of which is on page 155. And the Society for Psychical Research might give advice. Most of all a sceptical mind is needed, one that asks questions and takes nothing and no one for granted. Where ghosts are concerned, it is better to doubt that they exist at all than to believe in them unquestioningly, and in every story told about them.

To begin, then, at the beginning. Traditional folk tales and local stories are a rich deposit of material for a ghost hunter. They make entertaining reading, which alone is good enough reason for bothering with them. But they also help us get used to the less-than-half-true story. They help us to learn the signs of a narrative dressed up by story-tellers none too worried about accuracy and factual correctness and much more concerned about drama and effect. These are the tales that men have told in public bars at night for the amusement of their mates, and grandmothers have told their grandchildren as mildly frightening good-night stories. They are rounded, like pebbles in a stream, by years of wear, smooth and easy to listen to and hold in the imagination. And when we compare these few representative stories that follow in the next three chapters with the account of the ghost Miss Morton saw, as well as the descriptions in Chapter 5, we can see at once the difference between the fascinating symbolic truth of legend and the absorbing interest of observed events told as honestly as people can manage. If we are to understand ghosts and inquire into them, this is the first lesson we must learn: to recognize the truth of fiction and the truth of observed fact.

2 · The Ghost in the Fen

A fisherman's tale

This story is told in *More Tales from the Fens* by Mr W. H. Barrett. I have selected it partly because it amuses me but mostly because it is a good example of the kind of local tale you can hear anywhere in Britain. It is composed of a few grains of well-hidden truth and a lot of entertaining but quite fictional invention.

Ghosts, bor? Why, the old Fen's full of them. The best time to see them is during what we call chiming hours: four, eight and twelve o'clock. Have I seen any of them? Of course I have, and so will you if you live as I've done and spend five nights out of six poaching or fishing like I do. I used to go fishing in the finest swim for bream that there was in the river; it was down by that blasted ash tree just before you come to Littleport Chair [on the Ouse, north of Littleport]. Years ago there was a house quite close up to the bank there, but it's gone now.

One night I'd been fishing for hours without even getting a little nibble, let alone a bite. I'd just made up my mind to pack up and go home when the old boat started rocking and I wondered what was up. Then a pair of hands grabbed hold of the side, nearly upsetting me, and as I sat there, dumb-struck, I saw a lovely young woman clambering into the boat. She had long hair which came right down to her knees and that was all she had on to keep out the cold. I wasn't what you'd call scared, just a bit uncomfortable because I knew there was a chap fishing a bit higher up river and I didn't like the idea of him coming along and seeing a pretty young woman in the boat with me. So I asked her:

'What do you want, my gal?'

She shook her head, which made the water fly out of her hair; some of it got into my eyes, but, though it made them smart, I could still see what a white skin she had. I asked her again:

'What do you want?'

But before the words were out of my mouth she was overboard and in the river and back again with a baby in her arms. I told her she was a better hand at fishing than I was, as I'd been sitting there all night and not pulled out a thing, let alone a baby.

Well, she sat there for some time, nursing the little one, then I told her that, as my luck was out, I was pulling for home and bed — that is, unless she liked to nip over the side and bring back a few bream instead of a baby. Then the boat rocked so much that it flung me off the seat backwards and I got such a ding on the back of my head, as I hit the planks at the bottom, that I went right off to sleep, and lay there till the other chap came along and woke me by saying:

'Blast you, bor, I've been out all night and not had a bite, and here you are with so many fish that you got tired of pulling them out, and went to sleep.'

And do you know, when I looked down I saw more fish lying on the bilge boards than I could have caught in a week, and when I pulled out my keep-net, that was full too.

'Yes,' I said, 'I've had pretty good luck tonight; that's because I've had someone to help me, but she must have gone home a good while ago.'

'And time, too,' he said, 'for I reckon you and your old woman must have caught every fish in the river.'

Next day I went to see old Bob Newton, who was the oldest man in the Fen — near a hundred he must have been. I shouted into his ear, because he was very deaf:

'Bob, have you ever done any fishing up by the blasted ash?'

'Not for sixty years,' he said, 'because one night when I was fishing there — and I'll swear I was sober at the time — a young woman bobbed up out of the water and climbed into my boat, which I'd staked about four yards from the bank. I was so scared that I took one leap and landed on the bank and cut off home as hard as I could go. You see, I'd heard the old tale that, years ago, the daughter of the man who lived in the house that used to stand near that tree, came home from Cambridge, where she'd been in service, with a young baby in her arms. This made her father fly into such a rage that he hurled the pair of them into the river. All that was before my time, of course, so I can't say if it's true or not. But all the old-timers swear it's true, and that's why that stretch of river is so full of bream, because no one dares go fishing there at night."[1]

1. From W. H. Barrett, *More Tales from the Fens*; Routledge & Kegan Paul, 1964.

3 · The Hairy Hands

Hovering half way between fact and fiction is this story from *Legends of Devon* by J. R. W. Coxhead. The ghost is still supposed to be active as described in the narrative, but the legend is so old that everyone in the area knows it and you can be sure that any accident near the reputedly haunted spot will be blamed on the spectre. Take with a pinch of salt also the evidence of the 'psychic' woman. There are some people who will see anything once they know it is supposed to be there. The difference between self-deception and psychic power is sometimes difficult to be sure about.

One day in June 1921, Dr E. M. Helby, Medical Officer to the prison at Princetown, was riding on his motor-bicycle along the road which crosses Dartmoor from Two Bridges to Moretonhampstead.

In the sidecar attached to the machine there were two children. They were travelling down the slope towards the bridge which crosses the East Dart near Postbridge, when, according to an account given by the children afterwards, the doctor suddenly shouted out: 'There's something wrong. Jump!'

The next moment the bicycle swerved, the engine broke away from its fastenings and the doctor was hurled from his seat into the roadway. He landed on his head with such force that he was killed instantly. Luckily, the two children were unhurt.

On 26 August 1921, a young army officer left the house of a friend on a motor-bicycle, with the intention of visiting some people at a considerable distance. An hour later he returned to his friend's house, cut and bruised, his bicycle badly damaged. While he was having his hurts tended, his friend asked him to describe how the accident had happened. A queer look came into the young man's eyes, and he said:

'You will find it difficult to believe, but something drove me off the road. A pair of hairy hands closed over mine – I felt them as plainly as ever I felt anything in my life – large, muscular, hairy hands. I fought against them as hard as I could, but it was no use, they were too strong for me. They forced the machine into the side of the road, and I knew no more until I came to my senses lying on my face on the turf a few feet away from the bicycle.'

The spot where the accident occurred was close to the place where Dr Helby was killed earlier in the year.

In 1924, three years after the two accidents took place, a woman who is psychic saw one of the 'hairy hands' about a mile west of the place where the accidents occurred. She and her husband were in a caravan near the ruins of the Powder Mills, about half a mile to the north of the road. She awoke with a start one cold moonlit night, with a strong feeling that there was something highly dangerous close at hand. The following account of her terrifying experience is taken from the *Transactions of the Devonshire Association*, Vol. 82, p. 115:

'I knew there was some power very seriously menacing us near, and I must act swiftly. As I looked up to the little window at the end of the caravan, I saw something moving, and as I stared, my heart beating fast, I saw it was the fingers and palm of a very large hand, with many hairs on the joints and the back of it, clawing up and up to the top of the window, which was a little open.

'I knew it wished to do harm to my husband sleeping below. I knew that the owner of the hand hated us, and wished us harm, and I knew it was no ordinary human hand, and that no blow or shot would have any power over it. Almost unconsciously, I made the sign of the Cross and I prayed very much that we might be kept safe from harm.

'At once the hand slowly sank down out of sight, and I knew the danger had gone. I did say a thankful prayer, and fell at once into a peaceful sleep.

'We stayed in that spot several weeks, but I never felt the evil influence again near the caravan. But I did not feel happy in some places, not far off, and would not for anything have walked alone on the moor at night or the Tor above our caravan.'

. . . In the days of horse-drawn vehicles, the lonely road over the moor between Two Bridges and Moretonhampstead was greatly feared by benighted travellers because of the danger of a possible materialization of the dreaded spectral hands.

To the sceptical mind many questions are left unanswered by this story. What evidence was there that the doctor's accident had anything to do with ghostly hands? None is offered. And the young army officer: couldn't he have been using the hairy hands story to cover a stupid and embarrassing accident brought on himself by careless driving on a nasty bank? Of course, his explanation *could* be honest to the last word. But, *as reported*, doesn't his speech sound just too well-composed to be true? Does anyone in a state of shock after a road crash speak in such dramatically sculptured sentences? As for the psychic lady, she wakes in the night and sees a sight that *she might expect to see if the hairy hands legend were true*. She allays her fears by prayers, a natural and praiseworthy thing to do, and, what is more important, it worked: she felt reassured and could go back to sleep. Had she been sleeping in a room said to be haunted by a large spider with green eyes, she would no doubt have woken up in the middle of the night and 'seen' just such a creature. Though I have to admit that the hairy hands could exist (there is no evidence of a scientific kind that they do, but equally, there is none that they don't), I am making the point that I believe the 'psychic' lady was the kind of person whose worries and fears come before her as ghost-like figures which she truly believes she 'sees'. And those imagined figures take the shape of whatever ghost she hears about and which is supposed to haunt the place where she is at any one time. This is quite as likely as the possibility that she was indeed psychic and possessed the power of perceiving what others do not. The trouble is that the story does not supply any evidence which helps us to decide the truth about her. And so we have to say that, interesting though the story is, it is not very much use as evidence for or against the existence of ghosts, nor does it help us to understand them if they do exist.

4 · The Hideous Face with Flaming Eyes

According to legend, vampires are vicious, evil, and bloodthirsty. They are supposed to be corpses that rise from their graves, supernaturally brought back to inhuman life. And in order to stay alive, they must suck the blood of sleeping men and women. Once raised by whatever ugly powers reanimate them, there are only two ways of 'laying' these ghastly creatures: either by staking the offending corpses to the ground, impaling them through the heart, or by burning them.

Belief in such strange ghosts has always been more widespread in eastern Europe, Greece and China, than in Britain and the West. And I cannot say I take them very seriously myself. They belong to horror fiction, not to real life. If there is any explanation for belief in vampires, it probably has more to do with stories that start with gruesome murders or perhaps attacks on people at night by rabid animals, than with the supernatural.

But even if vampires belong only to over-excited imaginations, to the lurid world of nightmare and of groundless fears played upon by rumour and morbid fancies, they must be given a small place in a book about ghosts. For there are people who believe in them and who are haunted by the thought of their bloodsucking habits. So I have looked for accounts of British vampires, have found a few, and been convinced by none. But some are mildly entertaining and the one that follows comes from a book called *In My Solitary Life* by Augustus Hare. It concerns a place called

Croglin Grange in Cumberland, which was owned for hundreds of years by a family named Fisher. Some time ago, they moved out and rented the house to two brothers and their sister.

This new family settled quickly and happily into the life of the district, and soon became very popular. One hot summer day, when the sultry atmosphere had made work of any kind almost impossible, the three dined early, and afterwards sat out on the veranda, enjoying the cooler air, and watching the moon rise in full brilliance over the lawn and gardens.

When at last they went indoors to their rooms, the sister still felt the heat too great for sleep, and sat up in her bed, still watching the moonlight through her window, for she had not closed her shutters. Gradually she became aware of two lights which flickered in and out in the belt of trees which separated the lawn from the churchyard, and as her gaze became fixed upon them she saw them emerge, fixed in a dark substance, a definitely ghastly *something*, which seemed every moment to come nearer, increasing in size as it approached. Every now and then it was lost in the long shadows which stretched across the lawn, then it emerged larger than ever, and still coming on – on. She was seized with horror, and longed to get away, but the door was close to the window, and while unlocking it she must be for that instant nearer to *it*. She longed to scream, but her throat seemed paralysed.

Suddenly, she could never explain why, the terrible object seemed to turn aside, and to be going round the house, instead of straight towards her. She sprang from her bed to unlock the door, but at that instant she head a scratch, scratch, scratch at her window, and saw a hideous brown face with flaming eyes glaring in at her. She took comfort in the thought that the window was securely locked on the inside, but all of a sudden the scratching ceased, and a kind of pecking sound took its place. The creature was unpicking the lead! A diamond-shaped pane fell on to the floor, and a long bony finger came inside, and found the latch of the window, and turned it. She had fled back into her bed, but the creature came into the room, and twisted its long bony fingers into her hair, and dragged her head over the side of the bed, and bit her violently in the throat.

Now at last she did scream aloud, and her brothers rushed to her aid. But they had to break in the still-locked door, and by the time they got inside the creature had disappeared through the window, and their sister lay bleeding and unconscious. One brother tried in vain to pursue the monster, which vanished with gigantic strides, and seemed to disappear over the wall into the churchyard, so the pursuer returned to his sister's room. She was fearfully wounded, but recovered with amazing strength, and refused to let her terrible experience drive her from the house where they had been so happy. Both her doctor and her brothers, however, found it hard to believe that she could be so completely recovered as she seemed, and insisted on taking her away to Switzerland for a mental and physical change. There she threw herself into all the interests and occupations of the country, and seemed so fully restored to health that in the autumn she herself proposed that they should return to England. Her dreadful visitor, she maintained, must have been some escaped lunatic, and was not likely to return; besides, only one of the seven years for which they had leased their house had passed.

They therefore returned to Cumberland, but the sister always thereafter kept her shutters fast closed at night, and the two brothers each kept a loaded pistol in their room.

After a peaceful winter, in the following March the sister was suddenly awakened by the same dreadful scratching at her window, and saw the same hideous brown shrivelled face looking in through the one pane left uncovered at the top of the window by the shutters.

She screamed as loud as she could, and her brothers rushed with their pistols out of the house, to find the creature already scudding away over the lawn. One brother fired, and hit it in the leg, but it got away, nevertheless, and scrambled over the wall and seemed to disappear into a vault belonging to a family long extinct.

Next day, in the presence of all the tenants of Croglin Grange, this vault was opened, and a scene of horror presented itself; the coffins with which the vault was filled were all broken open save one, and their mangled contents scattered over the floor. On the last coffin the lid still lay, but it was loose, and when they raised it there lay inside, brown and withered but quite entire, the same frightful figure which had looked in at the window of the Grange, with the mark of a recent pistol-shot in one leg. They did the only thing that can lay a vampire – they burnt it.

PART TWO

Apparitions investigated

5 · Four Kinds of Ghost

Ghosts appear in all shapes and sizes and various shades of fearsomeness. Many, like good children years ago, can be seen but not heard, while others, the poltergeists, can be heard but not seen. Despite the differences between one ghost and another, however, there are ways of classifying them into groups of similar kinds. There are, for instance, hundreds of stories about transparent 'grey ladies' who glide silently through dark rooms in the middle of the night to the alarm of astonished percipients.[1] Then there are the spectral monks and nuns, the headless horsemen who gallop down ancient roads, the royal personages – the most popular being Anne Boleyn, who haunts a number of different places, though never, I think, all at the same time – the animals, and even a group of small ghostly children who are usually seen by old gentlemen, standing by their bedsides in a blaze of golden light. All these and more can be made into a catalogue of ghosts based upon the stories told about them.

But there is one very useful method of classifying apparitions if you are trying to understand the truth about these puzzling phenomena. The thousands of cases which have been reported to the Society for Psychical Research were carefully studied some years ago by an expert, Mr G. N. M. Tyrrell, who found that the accounts split into four very interesting classes. Sometimes, it is true, one ghost could quite comfortably fit into more than one

1. *Percipient:* The person to whom the experience is happening; the one who 'sees' the ghost.

class, but lepidopterists have the same trouble when classifying butterflies, and so do sociologists when studying people. No method is ever perfect. Mr Tyrrell's is the best when dealing with ghosts. So in this chapter I have tried to explain his four kinds of apparition, giving an example of each one just as he did in his book, *Apparitions*.

1 EXPERIMENTAL GHOSTS

People, it seems, do not have to be dead before their ghosts can appear. There are reports of ghosts being seen of people who are still alive and I have even come across a story of a man who claimed to have seen the ghost of himself! Not only this, but Mr Tyrrell found sixteen occasions when people decided to try and produce their own ghosts and make them appear before people a long way away who knew nothing about the 'experiment'. And they did so successfully.

These 'experimental ghosts' are very important, because if some people can make their ghosts appear just when and where they wish them to, then we have found a very useful way of studying apparitions. For if investigators knew when and where to expect an appearance, they could prepare cameras, tape recorders, thermometers and other specialized equipment with which to try and record what happened during the haunting. Yet strangely enough no one has ever followed up this possibility in a scientific manner. So here is a field of psychical research just waiting to be tackled by anyone properly trained to study it.

Mr Tyrrell chose the following account to illustrate what he meant by 'experimental' ghosts.

On Friday, December 1st, 1882, at 9.30 p.m., I went into a room alone and sat by the fireside, and endeavoured so strongly to fix my mind upon the interior of a house at Kew . . . in which resided Miss

V. and her two sisters, that I seemed to be actually in the house. During this experiment I must have fallen into a mesmeric sleep, for although I was conscious, I could not move my limbs. I did not seem to have lost the power of moving them, but I could not make the effort to do so, and my hands, which lay loosely on my knees, about six inches apart, felt involuntarily drawn together and seemed to meet, although I was conscious that they did not move.

At 10 p.m. I regained my normal state by an effort of the will, and then took a pencil and wrote down on a sheet of note-paper the foregoing statements. When I went to bed on this same night, I determined that I would be in the front bedroom of the above mentioned house at 12 midnight, and remain there until I had made my spiritual presence perceptible to the inmates of that room.

On the next day, Saturday, I went to Kew to spend the evening, and met there a married sister of Miss V., Mrs L. [The narrator had only met this lady once before.] In the course of conversation (although I did not think for a moment of asking her any questions on such a subject), she told me that on the previous night she had seen me distinctly on two occasions. She had spent the night at Clarence Road and had slept in the front bedroom. At about half-past nine she had seen me in the passage going from one room to another, and at about 12 p.m., when she was wide awake, she had seen me enter the bedroom and walk round to where she was sleeping, and take her hair (which is very long) into my hand. She also told me that the apparition took hold of her hand, and gazed intently into it, whereupon she spoke, saying, 'You need not look at the lines, for I have never had any trouble.' She then woke her sister, Miss V., who was sleeping with her and told her about it. After hearing this account, I took the statement, which I had written down on the previous evening, from my pocket, and showed it to some of the persons present, who were much astonished although incredulous ... I asked Mrs L. if she was not dreaming at the time of the latter experience, but this she stoutly denied, and stated that she had forgotten what I was like, but seeing me so distinctly she recognized me at once.

How is it possible for one person to make another see his ghost?

Has it something to do with TELEPATHY? And does the percipient actually see the ghost, or is what he sees more like a
dream, an image in his imagination which he for some unexplained reason *thinks* he sees before him? Questions like these
come to mind at once. But the one that teases my mind is the
most difficult of all to explain. In the account the narrator fixed
his mind on the house in Kew, a place he knew well, and concentrated so hard upon it that he fell into a kind of trance – 'a
mesmeric sleep'. Then, on going to bed, he willed himself to
appear in the front bedroom of the house, the room Mrs L. and
Miss V. slept in. So far, so good. It is not too difficult to believe
that such intense concentration of willpower might somehow
produce an 'impression' of the narrator – his 'ghost' – just where
he wanted it to appear. But *more than a vague impression* was
witnessed. Mrs L. saw the apparition behaving as though it were
a real, flesh-and-blood person actually present. It walked down
a passage looking into the rooms; and finally, coming into the
bedroom, went round the bed and (how frightening for Mrs L.!)
took her hair in its hand. Now as far as we know, the narrator
imagined none of this. In fact he had no idea that Mrs L. was in

---

TELEPATHY

Telepathy *literally means 'feeling at a distance'. We use
it as the name for communication between one person's mind and another's without the use of spoken
words or any other outward signs and symbols (such as
writing, or radio, or hand signals, etc.). Telepathy is
mind speaking directly to mind, and is what 'mind-
readers' are supposed to use.*

the bedroom at that time and so could hardly have willed his 'ghost' to take up her hair in its hand. What is the explanation for this extraordinary event? Does a 'ghost', once produced, behave as it wants to and not as its producer wants it to? Or are there facts about the circumstances of this experimental apparition we do not know and which would make clear why it behaved as it did? No one really knows the answers, and until carefully conducted investigations are carried out it is unlikely that we shall ever understand what went on. All we can say is that experimental ghosts have been produced which, in our present state of ignorance, is a shivery thought.

2 CRISIS GHOSTS

These apparitions, like those in class one, frequently belong to people who are alive as well as to those who are dead. What is common to them all is that they occur when the person to whom the ghost belongs is going through a great personal crisis – a time of extreme difficulty. The biggest crisis of all is, of course, death. So it is not surprising that most crisis ghosts are associated with that event in people's lives. And usually the ghost appears to a friend or relative, not to strangers. In order to separate crisis appearances from those in other groups, we have to decide how long before and after the crisis actually happens the apparition can appear for it to be classed as a crisis ghost. Mr Tyrrell and other experts agreed that twelve hours either side of the event would be the limits. Thus, if a man died in a car accident at four in the afternoon and his wife 'saw' his ghost at any time from four o'clock the morning before until four o'clock the morning after then it would count as a crisis appearance.

Here is a typical account of such an apparition. It is told by the step-sister of an airman shot down in France on 19 March

1917, early in the morning, at which time the percipient was in India.

My brother appeared to me on the 19th March 1917. At the time I was either sewing or talking to my baby – I cannot remember quite what I was doing at that moment. The baby was on the bed. I had a very strong feeling that I must turn round; on doing so I saw my brother, Eldred W. Bowyer-Bower. Thinking he was alive and had been sent out to India, I was simply delighted to see him, and turned round quickly to put baby in a safe place on the bed, so that I could go on talking to my brother; then turned round again and put my hand out to him, when I found he was not there. I thought he was only joking, so I called him and looked everywhere I could think of looking. It was only when I could not find him I became very frightened and the awful fear that he might be dead. I felt very sick and giddy. I think it was 2 o'clock the baby was christened and in the church I felt he was there, but I could not see him. Two weeks later I saw in the paper he was missing. Yet I could not bring myself to believe he had passed away.

Two things are striking about crisis ghosts. First of all, the percipients mistake them for real people, so normal and life-like do they look, just as the airman seemed to be to his sister. Secondly, they appear unexpectedly. The percipients are usually doing something quite unimportant, or are relaxing or are about to go to sleep, and are not thinking at all of the person whose ghost they suddenly see.

Might telepathy explain this kind of ghost? Might it be that at the time of death people think so strongly of those they love that they influence the minds of the percipients who then 'see' their image? And why is there sometimes a time lag between the event itself and the moment when the percipient 'sees' the ghost? Certainly, crisis apparitions affect the people who experience them very deeply, for they often describe them as being shattering and often faint or break into tears, or feel a sense of shock. They also remember the moment vividly for many years after it happens.

Crisis ghosts are so frequently reported that I'd like to quote another case, one which I find fascinating, and which has been carefully documented so that it is possible to be fairly sure that the people involved were not dreaming, or playing a hoax, or simply imagining that it all happened. Once again, the story concerns an airman, Lieutenant David M'Connel, and the first piece of evidence is a letter written by the officer's father to a famous psychical expert, Sir Oliver Lodge. Mr M'Connel relates how he first heard about his son's ghostly appearance, and then goes on:

16th January, 1919

The circumstances of the flight were as follows. My son, with other officers, had been to a dance at Lincoln on the night of the 6th December. He got up rather late on the morning of the 7th, missed parade, and also had no breakfast. The formal completion of all his tests for 'getting his wings' were to take place on the 7th. As the account states, he was on his way to start for the Aerial Range to shoot off those final tests when he was asked by the Officer Commanding to take one of two 'Camels' to Tadcaster. He went therefore unexpectedly, rather fatigued, and without food. I may say here that his O.C. considered him a 'born flyer' and that he was a very cautious and careful flyer, though not shirking necessary risks. By most unusual favour, he had been accepted for permanent service *before* he had won his 'wings' . . . The weather was fair when he left Scampton to fly to Tadcaster, a distance of 60 miles. He was accompanied by another 'Avro' plane – a 2-seater – which was to have brought him back to Scampton after delivery of the 'Camel'. You are probably aware that a 'Camel' scout plane is a notoriously difficult and sensitive one, and requires continued strain and effort to keep it down [flying properly]. At Doncaster the two planes ran into fog. My son and his Avro companion descended, and my son described the situation to his flight commander and asked for instructions by telephone. The reply was, 'Use your own discretion.' We suppose that my son's anxiety to finish his tests prompted him to continue.

His companion states that neither of them lunched at Doncaster. Between Doncaster and Tadcaster the fog became very thick. The Avro man had to come down, and made a forced landing, successfully. My son circled round him to see that he was all right and continued his flight to Tadcaster.

Sixty miles is not a long flight. But the fog was very dense. In order to keep touch with the solid [that is, to keep the ground in sight] a flyer has to keep his plane under such circumstances about 150 ft. above the surface of the ground – a feat in a 'Camel' of considerable difficulty. My son must have encountered difficulty, as he did not approach Tadcaster till nearly 3.30. Allowing for half or three-quarters of an hour for the descent at Doncaster, he must have been flying for about three and a quarter to three and a half hours on this occasion. I am told that it is as much as an ordinary flyer can do to fly a 'Camel' for two hours. The strain on the arms is intense. In fact, his mother, who saw his body on Monday 9th at midday, observed that his hands were tightly clenched and his forearms swollen.

As he at last approached Tadcaster Aerodrome, the machine was seen approaching by a man on the road about a quarter of a mile distant from the camp, who reported the fog to be extremely dense. During the evidence at the inquest a girl, or young woman, said she was watching the plane, and saw it apparently 'side-slip', then right itself. It flew steadily for a minute or two, then mounted suddenly and immediately 'nose-dived' and crashed. The engine was full on when the crash occurred. My son was thrown violently forward – his head striking the gun before him, which was not hooded. One arm was broken, one leg was torn. The girl ran to the spot and 'found the officer dead'. The violence of contact seems to have stopped his watch, which registered 3.25 p.m. His cigarette case was almost doubled up.

These are the circumstances of the accident, so far as I am aware of them. I am informed by flying men that the reaction on reaching safety after a difficult flight is so 'terrible' that fainting is not unknown. My son, it is thought, may have fainted; hence the crash, and his inability to save himself: or there was possibly engine trouble. I am also told that when shot, or in danger, the immediate thought of the flyer is usually a quite trivial one, such as the sudden desire for a cup of cocoa, or to get undressed at camp, etc. I mention this because the 'appearance' was not made at my son's home, or to his mother, who was there at the time, but in his own camp-room, and to a person who was a comparative stranger. However, his mother did have a strange impression at the hour of his death . . .

David R. M'Connel

Along with this very detailed account of his son's death, Mr M'Connel sent to Sir Oliver the following letter, written by Lieutenant J. J. Larkin, the man who saw Lieutenant M'Connel's apparition. Again this is detailed and very carefully composed, which is why it is such an interesting document in the study of crisis ghosts.

34 T.D.S. Royal Air Force, Scampton, Lincoln, December 22, 1918
David [M'Connel], in his flying clothes, about 11 a.m. went to the hangars intending to take a machine to the 'aerial range' for machine-gun practice. He came into the room again at 11.30 and told me that he did not go to the range, but that he was taking a 'Camel' to Tadcaster drome. He said, 'I expect to get back in time for tea. Cheerio.' He walked out and half a minute later, knocked at the window and asked me to hand him out his map, which he had forgotten.

After I had lunch, I spent the afternoon writing letters and reading, sitting in front of the stove fire. What I am about to say now is extraordinary to say the least, but it happened so naturally that at the time I did not give it a second thought. I have heard and read of similar happenings and I must say that I always disbelieved them absolutely. My opinion had always been that the persons to whom these appearances were given were people of a nervous, highly-strung, imaginative temperament, but I had always been among the incredulous ones and had been only too ready to pooh-pooh the idea. I was certainly awake at the time, reading and smoking. I was sitting as I have said, in front of the fire, the door of the room being about eight feet away at my back.

I heard someone walking up the passage; the door opened with the usual noise and clatter that David always made; I heard his 'Hello, boy!' and I turned half round in my chair and saw him standing in the doorway, half in and half out of the room, holding the door knob in his hand. He was dressed in his full flying clothes, but wearing his naval cap,[1] there being nothing unusual in his appearance. His cap was pushed back on his head and he was smiling, as he always was when he came into the rooms and greeted us.

In reply to his 'Hello, boy!' I remarked, 'Hello, back already?' He replied: 'Yes, got there all right, had a good trip.' I am not positively sure of the exact words he used, but he said, 'Had a good trip', or 'Had a fine trip', or words to that effect. I was looking at him the whole time he was speaking. He said, 'Well, cheerio!' closed the door noisily and went out.

I went on with my reading and thought he had gone to visit some friends in one of the other rooms, or perhaps had gone back to the hangars for some of his flying gear, helmet, goggles, etc., which he may have forgotten. I did not have a watch, so could not be sure of the time, but was certain it was between a quarter and half-past three, because shortly afterwards Lieut. Garner-Smith came into the room and it was a quarter to four. He said, 'I hope Mac (David) gets back early, we are going to Lincoln this evening.' I replied, 'He *is* back, he was in the room a few minutes ago.' He said, 'Is he having tea?' and I replied that I did not think so, as he (Mac) had not changed his clothes, but that he was probably in some other room. Garner-Smith said, 'I'll try and find him.'

---

1. An important detail. David M'Connel joined the R.A.F. from the Royal Navy and was proud of his former connection with the R.N. He always wore his naval cap when not on official duty, something only two other men did at Scampton at that time. It should also be remembered that when he took off earlier in the day, M'Connel was wearing not his naval cap but a flying helmet, and his father possessed a photograph taken just before David climbed into his 'Camel' plane which proved that this was so. – A.C.

I then went into the mess, had tea, and afterwards dressed and went to Lincoln. In the smoking-room of the Albion Hotel I heard a group of officers talking, and overheard their conversation and the words 'crashed' and 'M'Connel'. I joined them and they told me that just before they had left Scampton, word had come through that M'Connel had 'crashed' and had been killed taking the 'Camel' to Tadcaster. At that moment I did not believe it, that he had been killed on the Tadcaster journey. My impression was that he had gone up again after I had seen him, as I felt positive that I had at 3.30. Naturally I was eager to hear something more definite, and later in the evening I heard that he *had* been killed on the Tadcaster journey.

Next morning Garner-Smith and I had a long discussion about my experience. He tried to persuade me that I must have been mistaken, that I had not actually seen Mac on the previous afternoon about 3.30, but I insisted that I *had* seen him. As you can understand, Mr M'Connel, I was at a loss to solve the problem. There was no disputing the fact that he *had* been killed whilst flying to Tadcaster, presumably at 3.25, as we ascertained afterwards that his watch had stopped at that time. I tried to persuade myself that I had not seen him or spoken to him in this room, but I could not make myself believe otherwise, as I was undeniably awake and his appearance, voice and manner had all been so natural.

Jas. J. Larkin, 2nd Lt., R.A.F.

In a separate statement, Lieutenant Garner-Smith confirmed Lieutenant Larkin's account. After which the Society for Psychical Research asked Lieutenant Larkin to clear up some points, which he did in another letter. He was, he reported, quite sure that he saw the apparition between 3.20 and 3.30 p.m., that the room was quite small, about twelve feet square, that the electric light was on and the fire burning well in an open stove so that there were no shadows or half shadows, while outside it was still quite light even though the day was foggy and cold.

Bearing everything in mind, only one thing might explain what Lieutenant Larkin saw: that he mistook someone else for David

M'Connel. The obvious candidates for mistaken identity are the two other men who also wore naval caps. But, in the circumstances, this seems an unlikely solution. In a well-lit, small room, would Lieutenant Larkin confuse one man he knew well for another he knew well and with whom he had a conversation at a distance of but a few feet? Especially when, as was the case, the two other men who wore naval caps were not in height, build, behaviour or voice at all similar to the dead officer.

3 POST-MORTEM GHOSTS

Many stories tell of apparitions which the percipients recognize as belonging to people they once knew and who are now dead, but which appear so long after death that they cannot be classed as crisis ghosts. Their effect on the percipients is, however, frequently just the same: the ghosts appear suddenly and unexpectedly, are taken for living people so natural do they look, and often leave those who see them in a state of shock and amazement. Post-mortem (*after death*) apparitions also quite often seem to want to communicate a message or turn up at a difficult time in the percipients' lives, as if trying to help them. As Mrs P. and her husband discovered one night after going to bed.

Mrs P. was lying awake, waiting to attend to her baby, which lay in a cot at the bedside. The light was on in the room and the door was locked. In her own words, she described what then happened:

I was just pulling myself into a half sitting posture against the pillows, thinking of nothing but the arrangements for the following day, when, to my great astonishment, I saw a gentleman standing at the foot of the bed, dressed as a naval officer, and with a cap on his head having a projecting peak. The light being in the position [it was], the face was in shadow *to me*, and the more so that the visitor was leaning upon his arms which rested on the foot rail of the bed-stead. I was too astonished to be afraid, but simply wondered who it could be; and instantly touching my husband's shoulder (whose face was turned from me), I said, 'Willie, who is this?' ... Meanwhile the form, slowly drawing himself into an upright position, now said in a commanding yet reproachful voice, 'Willie, Willie!' I looked at my husband and saw that his face was white and agitated. As I turned towards him he sprang out of bed as though to attack the man, but stood by the bedside as if afraid, or in great perplexity, while the figure calmly and slowly moved *towards the wall* at right angles with the lamp ... As it passed the lamp, a deep shadow fell upon the room as of a material person shutting out the light from us by his intervening body, and he disappeared, as it were, into the wall.

My husband now, in a very agitated manner, caught up the lamp and, turning to me, said, 'I mean to look all over the house and see where he is gone.' I was by this time exceedingly agitated too, but, remembering that the door was locked, and that the mysterious visitor had not gone towards it at all, remarked, 'He has not gone out by the door!' But without pausing, my husband *unlocked* the door, hastened out of the room, and was soon searching the house.

While her husband was out of the room, Mrs P. thought of her brother who was in the navy. Could he, she wondered, be in some kind of trouble? Was that the cause of the apparition? When Mr P. returned, she asked him what he thought of this. No doubt to her surprise, Mr P. replied, 'Oh no, it was my father!' Her account continues, '*My husband's father had been dead fourteen years*: he had been a naval officer in his young life.'

Some weeks later, after becoming very ill, Mr P. told his wife that he had got into financial trouble, and that at the time the apparition appeared he was about to take the advice of a man who would probably have led him into even worse difficulties.

Was this apparition the ghostly spirit of Mr P's dead father returning to earth in order to try and help his troubled son? Many people would believe so. And certainly at first glance this is the explanation anyone might offer. But if we look more closely and try and understand what was going on in that apparently peaceful bedroom just *before* the ghost appears, a quite different conclusion might suggest itself.

Mrs P. tells her story in the order that the events took place. Like herself, therefore, we learn only at the end that her poor husband, lying by her side as she waited to tend their baby, was far from at peace in his mind. He was, in fact, worried. Very worried. Indeed, he was probably near his wits' end. And when people are in such a distressed state they usually want to tell someone close to them about their troubles. Mr P. had already sought help, but from a man he could not trust, a man who, Mr P. later confessed, would have got him into even deeper trouble. What was Mr P. to do? His instinct must have been to unburden himself to his wife, the person nearest and dearest to him. But how could he weigh her down with his problems and cause her pain and anxiety when she had their baby to look after and the house to run? Should he not keep quiet and try to sort things out alone? If only his father were still alive! What would he have said, and wouldn't he have helped?

Thoughts like these no doubt tumbled about in Mr P.'s head that night as he lay half way between wakefulness and sleep. And in those semi-conscious moments of life, problems seem far worse than they really are. Then the oppressed and desperate imagination can focus all its powerful energy in one direction, on one idea, or thought, or deep desire. Perhaps as he slipped towards uneasy sleep Mr P. fixed upon a picture of his father, a picture mixed up with a cry for help and a longing to tell his wife of all that troubled him.

Suppose, at any rate, that something like this went on in Mr P.'s mind that fateful night. What happened next is then possible to guess at. Mr P. was in a state like that of the man who produced the 'experimental' ghost. He was in a 'mesmeric sleep', and was a transmitter, sending out a picture linked to his desire for help. Mrs P., relaxed and untroubled, 'received' the picture, for she was the person her husband most wished to communicate with. And so she 'saw' a figure dressed in naval uniform standing at the foot of the bed. Surprised, she naturally drew the attention of her half-conscious husband to the apparition. Because the two people involved were now linked in telepathic communication, the picture image was being sent back and forth between them. So when Mr P. looked up he also 'saw' the 'ghost'. He acted as he then did because he had no idea that the apparition was actually the product of his own mind. He had not set out to produce a ghost for his wife (or himself) to see, as the man in the 'experimental' case did. And so it not only surprised him but frightened him too, for there were his secret thoughts suddenly come to life! In fact, of course, the whole thing was simply a drama acted out in his imagination and shared telepathically with his wife. The naval figure did not actually exist in the room. The mind was deceiving the eye.

Once the experience was over it preyed on Mr P., adding to his worries, until finally he became ill and he did what he knew all along he ought to do and wanted to do. He told his wife about their money problems.

Apart from guessing at Mr P.'s thoughts, nothing in this explanation is invented: it is all possible. It is possible, for example, for one person to communicate with another by what is called telepathy: it is also possible for a 'transmitted' picture to be 'seen' by the 'receiver' as if it were real and present in the room. We do not know very much about how this works, or why, or in what conditions. But, in my opinion, it is an explanation of post-mortem ghosts that gets nearer to the truth than any other I know of.

4 GHOSTS

We are left with ghosts which haunt particular places time and again, which are seen by many people who have no connection with those the ghosts represent, and which appear for many years after the death of their owners. These are the spectral apparitions which people usually mean when they talk of spooks and tell stories about haunted places. There are thousands of them, almost every village and town in Britain having its own collection. Many of these local tales are nothing more than legends, and as they are told, generation to generation, details get added to make the stories more frightening or more entertaining. But some cannot be so easily accounted for. Mr Tyrrell quotes the following report of one such haunting, but there were scores to choose from of equal interest. (An especially interesting one is discussed in Chapter 6.) The woman who tells the story lived in a detached house that was no more than twenty years old with her husband, step-daughter, two small children, and servants.

We had been there about three weeks when, about eleven o'clock one morning, as I was playing the piano in the drawing-room, I had the following experience: I was suddenly aware of a figure peeping round the corner of the folding doors to my left; thinking it must be a visitor, I jumped up and went into the passage, but no one was there, and the hall door, which was half glass, was shut. I only saw the upper half of the figure, which was that of a tall man with a very pale face and dark hair and moustache. The impression lasted only a second or two, but I saw the face so distinctly that to this day I should recognize it if I met it in a crowd. It had a sorrowful expression. It was impossible for anyone to come into the house without being seen or heard ... In the following August one evening about 8.30, I had occasion to go into the drawing-room to get something out of the cupboard, when, on turning round, I saw the same figure in the bay window, in front of the shutters, which were closed. I again saw only the upper part of the figure, which seemed to be in a somewhat crouching posture. The light on this occasion came from the hall and the dining-room and did not shine directly on the window; but I was able perfectly to distinguish the face and the expression of the eyes ...

Later in the same month I was playing cricket in the garden with my little boys. From my position at the wickets I could see right into the house through an open door, down a passage and through the hall as far as the front door. The kitchen door opened into the passage. I distinctly saw the same face peeping round at me out of the kitchen door. I again only saw the upper half of the figure. I threw down the bat and ran in. No one was in the kitchen. One servant was out and I found the other was in her bedroom ...

A little later in the year about 8 o'clock one evening, I was coming downstairs alone, when I heard a voice from the direction, apparently, of my little boys' bedroom, the door of which was open. It distinctly said, in a deep, sorrowful tone, 'I can't find it'. I called out to my little boys, but they did not reply, and I have not the slightest doubt that they were asleep; they always called out if they heard me upstairs. My step-daughter, who was downstairs in the dining-room, with the door open, also heard the voice, and, thinking it was me calling, cried out, 'What are you looking for?' We were extremely puzzled. The voice could not by any possibility have belonged to any member of the household. The servants were in the kitchen and my husband was out.

A short time after I was again coming downstairs after dark in the evening, when I felt a sharp slap on the back. It startled but did not hurt me. There was no one near me and I ran downstairs and told my husband and my step-daughter.

The step-daughter also saw the ghost, and one night when playing with her brother on the landing she looked over her shoulder and saw the face again. At that moment her brother said, 'There's a man on the landing.'

How do we explain this class of ghosts? That is the most difficult question of all. Renée Haynes suggests one possibility in Chapter 12, but there are others, too long and complicated to go into here. Readers who would like to find out more might begin by studying the book which has been of indispensable help to me in writing this chapter: Mr Tyrrell's *Apparitions*.

6 · Miss Morton Sees a Ghost

One day in June 1882 Miss Morton saw a ghost. She was nineteen years old at the time, and was to see the ghost on several more occasions during the next seven years. Being of a scientific turn of mind, however, she was not prepared to let the ghost come and go as it pleased without proper investigation. And so this cool-nerved young woman carried out a number of experiments and observed the apparition closely in an effort to discover precisely what kind of phenomenon it was.

News of the 'Morton Ghost' soon reached Mr F. W. H. Myers, an eminent expert in psychical research in those days. He visited the Morton home, talked to the father, Captain Morton, the family and servants. And finally, though with some difficulty and not until the haunting was over, he managed to persuade Miss Morton (who was by then, in 1892, a medical student) to write an account of the ghost and its activities. *Record of a Haunted House* by Miss R. C. Morton is still one of the most fascinating and useful documents in the study of apparitions.

Before I quote the important parts of the Record, letting Miss Morton tell her own story, it is necessary that some details about the people and the house involved should be understood. To begin with, Morton was not the family's real name. It was chosen, and the address of the house kept secret, in order to protect the family's identity. Miss Morton was, in fact, Miss Rosina Despard, and her father was Captain F. W. Despard. Shortly after the haunting ended, in 1895, Rosina qualified with honours as a medical doctor. In 1928 she retired to the Isle of Wight where she died in 1930 aged sixty-seven. She was first publicly identified as Miss Morton in 1948, and because it is by that name she is now best known, I have retained it in the rest of this account.

At the same time as Miss Morton's real name was revealed the address of the house was made known. It still stands today, a large, square, Victorian family house in its own grounds on the corner of Pittville Circus Road, Cheltenham; known to the Despards as Garden Reach, it is now called St Anne's. At the time of the haunting – and it seems to have changed little in external appearance – it was cut off from the main road by high railings and gates and a short sweep of driveway. On one side was another, similar, detached house; on the other side a small orchard cut off the second road. At the back there was a large garden, and a small cottage and some stables, neither then in use, stood at the bottom end. The house had been built in 1860, when it was bought from the builders by an Anglo-Indian, Mr Henry Swinhoe, who occupied it for the next sixteen years.

Now Mr Swinhoe is interesting, and a vital piece in the puzzle. Events that took place in the house during his tenancy might very well have had something to do with Miss Morton's experiences later. Or, of course, they might not!

The known facts are these: One August during Mr Swinhoe's stay (the year is not known), his wife, whom he loved passionately, died. He was so grief-stricken he took to drink to try and drown his sorrow, and apparently he had some success, for two years later he married again.[1] Before long, however, the second Mrs Swinhoe was a heavy drinker too, having caught the habit

1. This is the account given in the Record. According to Andrew Mackenzie in his book *Apparitions and Ghosts* (Arthur Barker, 1971), pp. 148–9, Mr Swinhoe's grand-daughter, Mrs Violet Rhodes James, claimed that Mr Swinhoe was led to drink by his second wife whom he discovered to be a heavy drinker during their honeymoon.

from her alcoholic husband. What's more, they were constantly quarrelling, sometimes violently. The main subjects of these arguments were the five young children, who belonged to Mr Swinhoe's first wife, and some jewellery, also the first Mrs Swinhoe's, which Mr Swinhoe was keeping for the children. In order to ensure the jewellery's safety Mr Swinhoe employed a carpenter to put it in a specially built cupboard fitted under the floorboards in the small front sitting-room (marked 'c' on the plan).

This second marriage seems to have gone from bad to worse. At any rate, the second Mrs Swinhoe finally left her drunken husband and went to live in Clifton, Bristol, never to set foot in the house again, not even a few months later when, on 14 July 1876, Mr Swinhoe died in the same small front room where he had hidden the jewels.

The second Mrs Swinhoe herself died on 23 September 1878, and was buried in a churchyard about a quarter of a mile from the house where she had lived so unhappily.

The house itself was sold soon after Mr Swinhoe's death to a Mr L. (his full name is unknown to me), an elderly man who completely redecorated the place before moving in with his wife. They had lived there for less than six months when Mr L. died – and in that same small sitting-room (c) where Mr Swinhoe kept the jewels and met his own sad end.

Mrs L. moved out after her husband's funeral, and the house remained empty for about four years before the Despards came on the scene. And from this point the strange story is best told in 'Miss Morton's' own calm, straightforward words.

The family consists of Captain M. himself; his wife, who is a great invalid, neither of whom saw anything; a married daughter, Mrs K., then about 26, who was only a visitor from time to time, sometimes with, but more often without, her husband; 4 unmarried daughters, myself, then aged 19, who was the chief percipient and now gives the

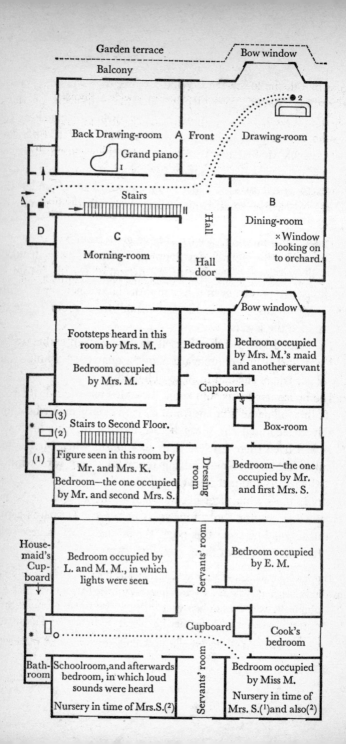

Garden terrace

Bow window

Balcony

Back Drawing-room   A   Front   Drawing-room

●2

Grand piano

I

Stairs

II

D

Hall

Hall
door

B

Dining-room

×Window
looking on
to orchard.

C

Morning-room

Bow window

Footsteps heard in this
room by Mrs. M.

Bedroom occupied
by Mrs. M.

Bedroom

Bedroom occupied
by Mrs. M.'s maid
and another servant

Cupboard

(3)

Stairs to Second Floor.

(2)

Box-room

(1)

Figure seen in this room by
Mr. and Mrs. K.

Bedroom—the one occupied
by Mr. and second Mrs. S.

Dressing
room

Bedroom—the one
occupied by Mr.
and first Mrs. S.

House-
maid's
Cup-
board

Bedroom occupied by
L. and M. M., in which
lights were seen

Servants' room

Bedroom occupied
by E. M.

Cupboard

Cook's
bedroom

Bath-
room

Schoolroom, and afterwards
bedroom, in which loud
sounds were heard

Nursery in time of Mrs.S.(2)

Servants' room

Bedroom occupied
by Miss M.

Nursery in time of
Mrs. S.(1) and also(2)

PLAN OF GROUND FLOOR
The two drawing-rooms are separated by a wide archway
formerly filled by folding doors.

1 Position of music stool, while sitting on which E. M. saw
figure behind her. 12/7/84.

2 Sofa on which figure sat, dot marking position behind, which
it took up when sofa was occupied.

■ Marks spot where figure usually disappeared.

‖ Marks position of mat.

.... Marks usual track of figure when followed downstairs,
into drawing-room, along passage to garden door, where it
disappeared.

Δ Garden door by which figure disappeared.

→ Shows direction in which doors open.

D Small lobby from which stairs go down to basement, and a
servants' staircase leads up to half-landing between ground and
first floors.

PLAN OF FIRST FLOOR

* Half-landing between ground floor and first floor.

(1) Door opening from servants' staircase.

(2) Stairs from ground floor.

(3) Stairs up to first floor.

PLAN OF SECOND FLOOR

* Half-landing between first and second floors.

o Marks position of figure when first seen by Miss M.

.... Marks course from Miss M.'s bedroom door to head of
stairs, where figure usually paused, looking towards bathroom
door, and then continued straight down the stairs, not stopping on
the first floor, and on the ground floor pursuing the course marked.

chief account of the apparition; E. Morton, then aged 18; L. and M. Morton, then 15 and 13; 2 sons, one of 16, who was absent during the greater part of the time when the apparition was seen; the other, then 6 years old.

My father took the house in March, 1882, none of us having heard of anything unusual about the house. We moved in towards the end of April, and it was not until the following June that I first saw the apparition.

I had gone up to my room, but was not yet in bed, when I heard someone at the door, and went to it, thinking it might be my mother. On opening the door, I saw no one; but on going a few steps along the passage, I saw the figure of a tall lady, dressed in black, standing at the head of the stairs. After a few moments she descended the stairs, and I followed for a short distance, feeling curious what it could be. I had only a small piece of candle, and it suddenly burnt itself out; and being unable to see more, I went back to my room.

The figure was that of a tall lady, dressed in black of a soft woollen material, judging from the slight sound in moving. The face was hidden in a handkerchief held in the right hand. This is all I noticed then; but on further occasions, when I was able to observe her more closely, I saw the upper part of the left side of the forehead, and a little of the hair above. Her left hand was nearly hidden by her sleeve and a fold of her dress. As she held it down a portion of a widow's cuff was visible on both wrists, so that the whole impression was that of a lady in widow's weeds [the black clothes worn by women mourning for their dead husbands]. There was no cap on the head but a general effect of blackness suggests a bonnet, with long veil or a hood.

During the next two years – from 1882 to 1884 – I saw the figure about half a dozen times; at first at long intervals, and afterwards at shorter, but I only mentioned these appearances to one friend, who did not speak of them to anyone.

During this period, as far as we know, there were only 3 appearances to anyone else.

1. In the summer of 1882 to my sister, Mrs K., when the figure

was thought to be that of a Sister of Mercy who had called at the house, and no further curiosity was aroused. She was coming down the stairs rather late for dinner at 6.30, it being then quite light, when she saw the figure cross the hall in front of her, and pass into the drawing-room. She then asked the rest of us, already seated at dinner, 'Who was that Sister of Mercy whom I have just seen going into the drawing-room?' She was told there was no such person, and a servant was sent to look; but the drawing-room was empty, and she was sure no one had come in. Mrs K. persisted that she had seen a tall figure in black, with some white about it; but nothing further was thought of the matter.

2. In the autumn of 1883 it was seen by a housemaid about 10 p.m., she declaring that someone had got into the house, her description agreeing fairly with what I had seen; but as on searching no one was found, her story received no credit.

3. On or about December 18th, 1883, it was seen in the drawing-room by my brother and another little boy. They were playing outside on the terrace, when they saw the figure in the drawing-room close to the window, and ran in to see who it could be that was crying so bitterly. They found no one in the drawing-room, and the parlourmaid told them that no one had come into the house.

After the first time, I followed the figure several times downstairs into the drawing-room, where she remained a variable time, generally standing to the right-hand side of the bow window. From the drawing-room she went along the passage towards the garden door, where she always disappeared.

The first time I spoke to her was on the 29th January, 1884. 'I opened the drawing-room door softly and went in, standing just by it. She came in past me and walked to the sofa and stood still there, so I went up to her and asked her if I could help her. She moved, and I thought she was going to speak, but she only gave a slight gasp and moved towards the door. Just by the door I spoke to her again, but she seemed as if she were quite unable to speak. She walked into the hall, then by the side door she seemed to disappear as before.' (Quoted from a letter written on January 31st.) In May

61

and June, 1884, I tried some experiments, fastening strings with marine glue across the stairs at different heights from the ground – of which I give a more detailed account later on.

I also attempted to touch her, but she always eluded me. It was not that there was nothing there to touch, but that she always seemed to be *beyond* me, and if followed into a corner, simply disappeared.

During these two years the only *noises* I heard were those of slight pushes against my bedroom door, accompanied by footsteps; and if I looked out on hearing these sounds, I invariably saw the figure. 'Her footstep is very light, you can hardly hear it, except on the linoleum, and then only like a person walking softly with thin boots on.' (Letter on January 31st, 1884.) The appearances during the next two months – July and August, 1884 – became much more frequent; indeed they were then at their maximum, from which time they seem gradually to have decreased, until now they seem to have ceased.

Of these two months I have a short record in a set of journal letters written at the time to a friend. On July 21st I find the following account. 'I went into the drawing-room, where my father and sisters were sitting, about 9 in the evening, and sat down on a couch close to the bow window. A few minutes after, as I sat reading, I saw the figure come in at the open door, cross the room and take up a position close behind the couch where I was. I was astonished that no one else in the room saw her, as she was so very distinct to me. My youngest brother, who had before seen her, was not in the room. She stood behind the couch for about half an hour, and then as usual walked to the door. I went after her, on the excuse of getting a book, and saw her pass along the hall, until she came to the garden door, where she disappeared. I spoke to her as she passed the foot of the stairs, but she did not answer, although as before she stopped and seemed as though *about* to speak.' On July 31st, some time after I had gone up to bed, my second sister E., who had remained downstairs talking in another sister's room, came to me saying that someone had passed her on the stairs. I tried then to persuade her that it was one of the servants, but next morning found it could not have been so, as none of them had been out of their rooms at that hour, and E.'s more detailed description tallied with what I had already seen.

On the night of August 1st, I again saw the figure. I heard the footsteps outside on the landing about 2 a.m. I got up at once, and went outside. She was then at the end of the landing at the top of the stairs, with her side view towards me. She stood there some minutes, then went downstairs, stopping again when she reached the hall below. I opened the drawing-room door and she went in, walked across the room to the couch in the bow window, stayed there a little, then came out of the room, went along the passage, and disappeared by the garden door. I spoke to her again, but she did not answer.

On the night of August 2nd the footsteps were heard by my three sisters and by the cook, all of whom slept on the top landing – also by my married sister, Mrs K., who was sleeping on the floor below. They all said the next morning that they had heard them very plainly pass and repass their doors. The cook was a middle-aged and very sensible person; on my asking her the following morning if any of the servants had been out of their rooms the night before, after coming to bed, she told me that she had heard these footsteps before, and that she had seen the figure on the stairs one night when going down to the kitchen to fetch hot water after the servants had come up to bed. She described it as a lady in widow's dress, tall and slight, with her face hidden in a handkerchief held in her right hand. Unfortunately we have since lost sight of this servant; she left us about a year afterwards on her mother's death, and we cannot now trace her. She also saw the figure outside the kitchen windows on the terrace-walk, she herself being in the kitchen; it was then about 11 in the morning, but having no note of the occurrence, I cannot now remember whether this appearance was subsequent to the one above mentioned.

These footsteps are very characteristic, and are not at all like those of any of the people in the house; they are soft and rather slow, though decided and even. My sisters would not go out on the landing after hearing them pass, nor would the servants, but each time when I have gone out after hearing them, I have seen the figure there.

On August 5th I told my father about her and what we had seen and heard. He was much astonished, not having seen or heard anything himself at that time – neither then had my mother, but she is slightly deaf and is an invalid.

He made inquiries of the landlord (who then lived close by) as to whether he knew of anything unusual about the house, as he had himself lived in it for a short time, but he replied that he had only been there for three months, and had never seen anything unusual.

On August 6th, a neighbour, General A., who lived opposite, sent his son to inquire after my married sister, as he had seen a lady crying in our orchard, which is visible from the road. He had described her to his son, and afterwards to us, as a tall lady in black, and a bonnet with a long veil, crying, with a handkerchief held up to her face. He did not know my sister by sight, as she had been with us a few days, and had been out very little, but he knew that she was mourning for her baby son. My sister was not in the orchard that day at all, is rather short, and wore no veil . . .

The same evening this General A. came over to our house, and we all took up various stations on the watch for the figure, which, however, was not seen by anyone.

That night my brother-in-law and sister distinctly heard footsteps going first up the stairs and then down. This was about 2 a.m.

On the evening of August 11th we were sitting in the drawing-room, with the gas lit but the shutters not shut, the light outside getting dusk, my brothers and a friend having just given up tennis, finding it too dark; my eldest sister, Mrs K., and myself both saw the figure on the balcony outside, looking in at the window. She stood there some minutes, then walked to the end and back again, after which she seemed to disappear. She soon after came into the drawing-room, when I saw her, but my sister did not.

The same evening my sister E. saw her on the stairs as she came out of a room on the upper landing.

The following evening, August 12th, while coming up the garden, I walked towards the orchard, when I saw the figure cross the orchard, go along the carriage drive in front of the house, and in at the open side door, across the hall and into the drawing-room, I following. She crossed the drawing-room, and took up her usual position behind the couch in the bow window. My father came in soon after, and I told him she was there. He could not see the figure, but went up to where I showed him she was. She then went swiftly round behind him, across the room, out of the door, we both following her. We looked out into the garden, having first to unlock the garden door, which my father had locked as he came through, but saw nothing of her.

On August 12th, about 8 p.m., and still quite light, my sister E. was singing in the back drawing-room. I heard her stop abruptly, come out into the hall, and call me. She said she had seen the figure in the drawing-room, close behind her as she sat at the piano. I went back into the room with her, and saw the figure in the bow window in her usual place. I spoke to her several times, but had no answer. She stood there for about 10 minutes or a quarter of an hour; then went across the room to the door, and along the passage, disappearing in the same place by the garden door.

My sister M. then came in from the garden, saying she had seen her coming up the kitchen steps outside. We all three went into the garden, when Mrs K. called out from a window on the first storey that she had just seen her pass across the lawn in front, and along the carriage drive towards the orchard. This evening, then, altogether 4 people saw her. My father was then away, and my youngest brother was out.

On the morning of August 14th the parlourmaid saw her in the dining-room, about 8.30 a.m., having gone into the room to open the shutters. The room is very sunny and even with all the shutters closed it is quite light, the shutters not fitting well, and letting sunlight through the cracks. She had opened one shutter when, on turning round, she saw the figure cross the room. We were all on the lookout for her that evening, but saw nothing; in fact, whenever we made arrangements to watch, and were especially expecting her, we never saw anything ...

On August 16th I saw the figure on the drawing-room balcony, about 8.30 p.m. She did not afterwards come into the room, as on the former occasion. On looking out at the side door, nothing could be seen.

The gardener said that he had seen the figure on the balcony that morning early, about 6 o'clock.

On August 19th, 3 days after, we all went to the seaside, and were away a month, leaving three servants in the house.

When we came back they said that they had heard footsteps and noises frequently, but as the stair-carpets were up part of the time and the house was empty, many of these noises were doubtless due to natural causes, though by them attributed to the figure.

The cook also spoke of seeing the figure in the garden, standing by a stone vase on the lawn behind the house.

During the rest of that year and the following, 1885, the apparition was frequently seen through each year, especially during July, August, and September. In these months the three deaths took place, viz.: Mr S. on July 14th, 1876, the first Mrs S. in August, and the second Mrs S. on September 23rd.

The apparitions were of exactly the same type, seen in the same places and by the same people, at varying intervals.

The footsteps continued, and were heard by several visitors and new servants, who had taken the places of those who had left, as well as by myself, 4 sisters and brother; in all about 20 people, many of them not having previously heard of the apparition or sounds.

Other sounds were also heard in addition which seemed gradually to increase in intensity. They consisted of walking up and down on the second-floor landing, of bumps against the doors of the bedrooms, and of the handles of the doors turning. The bumps against the bedroom doors were so marked as to terrify a new servant, who had heard nothing of the haunting, into the belief that burglars were breaking into her room, while another servant, who had a slight attack of facial hemiplegia [Bell's palsy, a temporary paralysis of facial nerves], attributed it to terror caused by attempts at her door worse than usual one night; the doctor, however, thought the attack was caused by cold rather than fright.

A second set of footsteps was also heard, heavy and irregular, constantly recurring, lasting a great part of the night, often 3 or 4 times a week. On the first floor the same noises are heard, especially in the front right-hand room formerly used by Mr and Mrs S.

Louder sounds were also heard in the summer of 1885, heavy thuds and bumpings, especially on the upper landing.

These facts were kept quiet, on account of the landlord, who feared they might depreciate the value of the house, and any new servants were not told of them, though to anyone who *had* already heard of them we carefully explained the harmless nature of the apparition. Some left us on account of the noises, and we never could induce any of them to go out of their rooms after they had once gone up for the night.

During this year, at Mr Myers' suggestion, I kept a photographic camera constantly ready to try to photograph the figure, but on the few occasions I was able to do so, I got no result; at night, usually only by candle-light, a long exposure would be necessary for so dark a figure, and this I could not obtain. I also tried to communicate with the figure, constantly speaking to it and asking it to make signs, if not able to speak, but with no result. I also tried especially to *touch* her, but did not succeed. On cornering her, as I did once or twice, she disappeared . . .

In the course of the following autumn we heard traditions of earlier haunting, though, unfortunately, in no case were we able to get a first-hand account . . .

We also now heard from a carpenter who had done jobs in the house in Mrs S.'s time, that Mrs S. had wished to possess herself of the first Mrs S.'s jewels. Her husband had called him in to make a receptacle under the boards in the morning-room on the ground floor, in which receptacle he placed the jewels, and then had it nailed down and the carpet replaced. The carpenter showed us the place. My father made him take up the boards; the receptacle was there, but empty.

My father thought that there might be something hidden near the garden door, where the figure usually disappeared. The boards were taken up, and nothing was there but the original shavings and dust . . .

During 1887 we have few records; the appearances were less frequent ... During the next two years, 1887 to 1889, the figure was very seldom seen, though footsteps were heard; the louder noises had gradually ceased.

From 1889 to the present, 1892, so far as I know, the figure has not been seen at all; the lighter footsteps lasted a little longer, but even they have now ceased.

The figure became much less substantial on its later appearances. Up to about 1886 it was so solid and life-like that it was often mistaken for a real person. It gradually became less distinct. At all times it intercepted the light; we have not been able to ascertain if it cast a shadow.

These are the most interesting parts from 'Miss Morton's' extraordinary story. She ended her account with some general comments. First of all she listed her reasons for thinking that the ghost really was a ghost and not an ordinary flesh-and-blood person (she called these 'Proofs of Immateriality'). She next gave some reasons for supposing that the apparition might belong to the second Mrs Swinhoe. Then she reported on the behaviour of the animals in the house, before describing her feelings when the figure appeared.

PROOFS OF IMMATERIALITY

1. I have several times fastened fine strings across the stairs at various heights before going to bed, but after all others have gone up to their rooms ... They were knocked down by a very slight touch, and yet would not be felt by anyone passing up or down the stairs, and by candle-light could not be seen from below. They were put at various heights from the ground, from 6 inches to the height of the banisters, about 3 feet.

I have twice at least seen the figure pass through the cords, leaving them intact.

2. The sudden and complete disappearance of the figure, while still in full view.

3. The impossibility of touching the figure. I have repeatedly followed it into a corner, when it disappeared, and have tried to suddenly pounce upon it, but have never succeeded in touching it or getting my hand up to it, the figure eluding my touch.

4. It has appeared in a room with the doors shut.

On the other hand, the figure was not called up by any desire to see it, for on every occasion when we had made special arrangements to watch for it, we never saw it. On several occasions we have sat up at night hoping to see it, but in vain ... Nor have the appearances been seen after we have been talking or thinking much of the figure.

The figure has been connected with the second Mrs S.; the grounds for which are:

1. The complete history of the house is known, and if we are to connect the figure with any of the previous occupants, she is the only person who in any way resembled the figure.

2. The widow's garb excludes the first Mrs S.

3. Although none of us had ever seen the second Mrs S., several people who *had* known her identified her from our description. On being shown a photo-album containing a number of portraits, I picked out one of her sister as being most like that of the figure, and was afterwards told that the sisters were much alike.

4. Her step-daughter and others told us that she especially used the front drawing-room in which she continually appeared, and that her habitual seat was on a couch placed in a similar position to ours.

5. The figure is undoubtedly connected with the house, none of the percipients having seen it anywhere else, nor had any other hallucination.

CONDUCT OF ANIMALS IN THE HOUSE

We have strong grounds for believing that the apparition was seen by two dogs.

1. A retriever who slept in the kitchen was on several occasions found by the cook in a state of terror, when she went into the kitchen in the morning – being a large dog, he was not allowed upstairs; he was also seen more than once coming from the orchard thoroughly

cowed and terrified. He was kindly treated and not at all a nervous dog.

2. A small skye-terrier, whom we had later, was allowed about the house; he usually slept on my bed, and undoubtedly heard the footsteps outside the door. I have notes of one occasion, on October 27th, 1887. The dog was then suffering from an attack of rheumatism, and very disinclined to move, but on hearing the footsteps it sprang up and sniffed at the door.

Twice I remember seeing this dog suddenly run to the mat at the foot of the stairs in the hall, wagging its tail, and moving its back in the way dogs do when expecting to be caressed. It jumped up, fawning as it would do if a person had been standing there, but suddenly slunk away with its tail between its legs, and retreated, trembling, under a sofa. We were all strongly under the impression that it had seen the figure. Its action was peculiar, and was much more striking to an onlooker than it could possibly appear from a description ...

In conclusion, as to the *feelings* aroused by the figure, it is very difficult to describe them; on the first few occasions, I think the feeling of awe at something unknown, mixed with a strong desire to know more about it, predominated. Later, when I was able to analyse my feelings more closely, and the first novelty had gone off, I felt conscious of a feeling of loss, as if I had lost power to the figure.

Most of the other percipients speak of feeling a cold wind, but I myself have not experienced this.

The record is signed, and dated 1 April 1892. A number of letters from other people who saw the apparition add more details to those given by 'Miss Morton' and confirm the truthfulness of her account. The full record, from which I have quoted, can be found in the *Proceedings* of the Society for Psychical Research, Vol VIII, part xxii, first published in 1892.

In understanding apparitions we are like a man from the days of Queen Elizabeth the First who by some accident of history happened to see a television programme. He would know he had seen something very strange and perhaps a little frightening, yet something 'real' that undoubtedly existed and was not just a day-dream. But he would be hard put to it to explain exactly what he had seen or how it was created. He could only do what 'Miss Morton' did very well: describe as honestly as he could what had happened to him. 'Miss Morton's' ghost is a classic of its kind – one of Mr Tyrrell's 'Class 4' kind, in fact (see page 52). It might well be called a 'true ghost': not a hoax, not the figment of 'Miss Morton's' imagination, but a phenomenon similar to those seen by many other people, but which we do not yet know enough about to explain.

7 · Caught by the Camera?

There is a saying: the camera never lies. A photograph, we tend to think, is a straightforward record of what the camera 'saw'. Unlike the human mind, it cannot invent what isn't there; it cannot see visions and dream dreams. It doesn't suffer from hallucinations, nor receive telepathic pictures and see them as apparitions. Surely then, if a ghost could be photographed, we would have indisputable proof that such phenomena exist? Perhaps – so long as it is true that the camera never lies.

With that idea in mind, many people have set out – and still do – to get a snapshot of an apparition. Their first problem, however, is to find a ghost that's willing to be caught by the camera. No easy problem to solve! As I've said before in this book, ghosts don't like keeping appointments and are very unco-operative with anyone who deliberately tries to meet them. You can sit for hours night after night in a well-known haunted spot and see nothing out of the ordinary. Then, the very next night after you've given up in despair, someone who knew nothing about ghosts haunting the place gets the fright of his life and sees everything in nerve-shattering detail. Not surprisingly, therefore, most pictures of ghosts have been taken by accident: they are 'spontaneous' photographs. The photographers were not looking for apparitions, and usually did not know until the pictures were developed what their cameras had 'seen'. *For they themselves usually saw nothing exceptional at the time.* (Keep this point in mind – it is important in a moment.)

A very good example of this sort of accident is the photograph of what looks like a figure kneeling in front of the altar in St Mary's Church, Woodford, Northamptonshire (see Plate 2). First published in the *People* newspaper on 3 July 1966, it was taken by an eighteen-year-old clerk called Gordon Carroll. In a sworn statement he said that he was the only person in the church at the time when the picture was exposed and he was amazed, when the film was developed, to see the figure before the altar. Mr Carroll told the newspaper:

I've always been interested in old houses, churches and castles and I've taken more than a thousand pictures in the last two or three years. Woodford Church is a very ancient place. There was a church there before the Normans came to England. It was mentioned in the Doomsday Book.

Anyway, I set up my camera – an Ilford Sportsman Rangefinder, which was almost brand-new – on a tripod. I used an Agfa CT 18 film to take pictures of coloured windows and took half-a-dozen other pictures of the church. Conditions were not perfect but I managed to get some very good slides of the windows.

I sent them off to be developed and when they came back the light had got at one I had taken of the altar. But when I put it through the projector I saw that I had taken the picture of a monk kneeling at the altar.

Was Gordon Carroll's first thought – that 'the light had got at' the film – correct? Or is the hazy shape really a photograph of an apparition? And if it is, why should the camera be able to 'see' what Gordon Carroll's eyes could not? Are we to believe photographic chemicals have psychic powers not given to human beings? This is why I said we should keep in mind the fact that in most cases of 'spontaneous' photographs the photographers saw nothing odd. If we accept that they really have taken pictures of ghosts, we must somehow explain why they did not see what a machine and some chemicals managed to record.

Certainly, other people claim similar results to Gordon Carroll's while innocently taking photos. The Marquis of Ely has in his possession a picture he took at a house in Bryanston Square, London, in 1936. No one present – the Marquis himself, his assistant, and the woman being photographed sitting beside a very fine marble fireplace – noticed anything ghostly. But when the picture was developed there on the extreme right-hand edge, and apparently walking out of view, was a black shape that looked for all the world like a woman dressed in old-fashioned clothes.

An even more remarkable shot was taken at the National Maritime Museum, Greenwich. While looking round the museum in 1966, a Canadian tourist and his wife, the Reverend and Mrs R. W. Hardy, decided to photograph the much-admired Tulip Staircase in the Queen's House. According to the Hardys no one was on the stairs just then. But the film, developed only after they had returned home, shows in astonishingly clear but nevertheless ghost-like detail two cowled, monkish figures climbing the stairs, each one holding the banister with the left hand, on which shines a ring. If this picture is a fake, it is an extremely clever one, and experts who have examined the original can detect no sign of fraud. There is a sequel to the story. In 1967 the Hardys returned to England and were interviewed by Mr Richard Howard of the Ghost Club, who was satisfied that the Hardys were unlikely to have deliberately set out to deceive. Later, members of the Ghost Club arranged a ghost hunt at the museum. No one saw anything PARANORMAL; but unexplained sounds were heard: footsteps, someone crying, voices, muttering, a bell that gave just one, lonely peal.

A notable exception to these 'spontaneous' pictures taken by a photographer unaware of what he is doing occurred at Raynham Hall, Norfolk, on 19 September 1936 (see Plate 4). Mr Indra Shira and his assistant, Captain Provand, were taking shots of various parts of the beautiful old house, which is famous for the

Brown Lady that haunts it. In the afternoon the men set up their equipment to photograph the oak main staircase. Captain Provand took a flashlight exposure and was preparing the camera to take another when Mr Shira saw, he said later, a luminous but transparent figure gliding down the stairs towards him. Despite his natural astonishment, he kept his presence of mind sufficiently to call out to his colleague and to press the exposure trigger. Provand had no time to look up until the photograph had been taken; and then nothing extraordinary was to be seen. The figure had vanished. Mr Shira, however, was quite sure they had snapped a ghost, and laid a bet with Captain Provand that it would show up when the picture was processed. And it did. Or, at least, a cloudy shape, resembling a woman dressed in a long, flowing gown, appeared on the photograph. Expert examination found nothing to suggest tampering at any stage, and the picture was reproduced in the magazine *Country Life*.

PARANORMAL

Para *means 'beyond' or 'aside from'. Thus,* paranormal *means aside from or beyond normal explanation. Paranormal events seem to break the known laws of nature. We know, for example, that people cannot walk through solid brick walls. When we see a ghost walk through a wall we say we have seen a 'paranormal phenomenon'. Of course, as soon as we understand how something happens and can detect the 'laws' that govern it, we tend to include it in what we think is normal. Thus, if we understood about ghosts and apparitions we would probably stop calling them paranormal phenomena.*

At first sight, evidence of this kind is very impressive. Unfortunately, a little thought will show how difficult it is to accept as conclusive proof that ghosts exist and materialize so that human beings (and cameras) can see them. The plain truth is that, though the camera may not lie, it does occasionally misbehave. We have to remember that it is nothing more than a piece of mechanical apparatus designed to pick up rays of reflected light and focus them on material coated with light-sensitive chemicals on which they are recorded in a pattern that we recognize as a representation (a picture) of something we see in reality. (The word *photography* means *writing* or *drawing with light*.) Many things, not all of them easily detected, can accidentally go wrong. The chemicals on the film may be faulty. Unwanted light may get into the camera before, during or after exposure. The photographer may, without knowing it, wrongly adjust the delicate controls, thus producing ghostly and unexpected effects. The developing process may not be properly handled. Conditions of light unnoticed by the photographer as he takes the picture (cross-lighting, reflection from glass or water or highly polished furniture, for example) may 'baffle' the lens, causing strange shapes to fall on the film behind. These are just a few of the more obvious possibilities; any one of them could cause an effect that looks ghostly to appear on the printed picture. And one thing we know about human beings is that when they see a shape their immediate instinct is to try and recognize a pattern in it. What's more, the human brain has the ability to fill in details missing from a shape but needed to make it resemble something known. Look, as a test, at this: h*me, d*g, b*d, g*os*. Anyone who can read this book is very likely to see in these incomplete collections of letters the words *home*, *dog*, *bed*, and *ghost*. D*g, of course, might also be *dig* or *dug*, and b*d might be *bad*, *bid*, *bod*, or *bud* while g*os* could be *goose*. But everyone will have tried to make one word at least from the letters in each combination. The same thing happens when we hear sounds and see shapes.[1]

People tend to see what they want to see, and what their minds have been prepared to see. If ghosts interest us, then when we see a hazy patch on a piece of film we begin almost automatically to wonder if it might be an apparition. We wish it was, and our brains try to supply what we wish to see. Of course, it is also true that people tend not to see what they do not wish to see: the eye and brain can 'cut out' what is actually present in front of us. Everyone has had the experience of searching for an object that seems to be lost. We look where we expect to find it, and then where we think it is less likely to be. After a number of attempts 'looking everywhere', as we say, we suddenly come across the lost object lying in clear view. We wonder how we can possibly have missed seeing it before. The fact is that we probably did not expect it to be where it actually was. So we 'cut it out of view'. This is something artists and scientists are constantly battling against: the 'bias' of the mind to see what it wants to see and not what it doesn't. So just as people who want to see ghosts can make them up out of ordinary shadows in a poorly lit room, and patches of light in a picture, others can see nothing where a solid object stands right in their path.

How does this affect 'spontaneous' photographs of ghosts? All we can actually say, if we are looking for the truth, is that they have on them arrangements of light and dark *which make us think of ghosts*. In order to reach a firm conclusion about the cause of those shapes and what they mean, if anything, we need

1. There is now a machine which can do this. It is a device that clears up poor television reception by filling in the bits of the picture on the screen which have been 'lost' or blurred because of interference. The TV reception from the last two manned space-shots to the moon were better than pictures received from previous expeditions because this machine was used.

to know a great deal more about them than we ever can know. We can never know, because it is always too late. It has all happened before anyone was aware of what was going on, and so could record details like the conditions in which the picture was taken, the make, type and condition of the camera, the aperture of the lens used and the speed of exposure, the make and quality of the film – and all the information about its processing – when it was developed, the temperature, the make of the substances, the equipment used. And even given all these, it would still be possible for accidental error to creep in unnoticed.

So much for 'spontaneous' photographs. They are of fascinating interest but provide little hope of proof that ghosts exist. What, then, about pictures taken by 'spirit mediums' – people who usually claim the power of 'seeing' spirits and set out to photograph them? Some have said they were successful.

In 1922 Mrs Ada Emma Deane, a charwoman whose hobby was photography, startled the world by producing a picture which showed, she said, and many believed her, the faces of the 'spirits' of dead soldiers (see Plate 5). This paranormal portrait, she told her admirers, of whom there were a great many, she had taken at the Cenotaph in London on Armistice Day (11 November – the anniversary of the end of World War 1). Within weeks Mrs Deane was famous. She was also on the way to a fortune, for she suddenly found herself able to photograph the spirit of any dead soul whose living relatives or friends paid her to do so. For three years she ran a lucrative business as a 'spirit photographer'. And each Armistice Day she repeated her original amazing feat by publishing yet another photograph crowded with the faces of war heroes slain years before in the defence of their country. Sadly for the celebrated Mrs Deane – though happily for everyone else – in 1924 a sharp-eyed employee of the Topical Press Agency noticed a surprising resemblance between Mrs Deane's soldier spirits and the photographs of footballers and sportsmen, all very much alive and kicking, published by the Agency. It was more than a chance resemblance, it seems. For when a statement to this effect was printed in the *Daily Sketch* newspaper Mrs Deane's Armistice Day pictures appeared no more. She was, to be blunt, a fraud, and not a very skilful one at that.

Fraud encourages fraud; there's always someone ready to copy and, if possible, improve on any venture, successful and honest or otherwise. Inspired, no doubt, by the daring charwoman, two Edinburgh laddies called Falconer produced in 1925 their own version of the Armistice Day parade of ghosts. Their gullible mother, a member (indeed, the founder) of the local Psychic Centre, blind to her young sons' deception, sent their photograph to the Society for Psychical Research along with a message. The picture, Mrs Falconer reported, had been taken 'on Armistice Day during the two-minute silence by my two boys who are both photographic mediums. A number of soldier boys in the group have been recognized.' (A case again of people seeing what they want to see.) The picture was, in fact, nothing less than a photograph of a number of other photographs of people's faces cut out and surrounded with cottonwool. The cottonwool looked – or was intended to look – like ethereal clouds through which the spirit faces peered. Its real use was to hide the cut-out edges of the pictures. Only someone who very deeply wanted to believe that what she saw was a record of psychical phenomena could possibly say of such a crude fake, as Mrs Falconer did: 'This photo reveals, in a most convincing manner, the continuity of life.'

This deep desire, felt by many people, to believe in an after-life, and their even greater desire to have their belief proved true beyond possible doubt, bedevils all psychical research. Because of it, otherwise intelligent and clear-thinking people allow themselves to accept without question barefaced lies and obvious fraud. Ever since the camera became commercially useful in the second half of the last century right up to the present day, un-scrupulous photographers have made easy money out of those who seek reassurance about life after death.

The original crook who exploited this impulse was an engraver and amateur photographer called William H. Mumler. He produced the first known 'spirit' photo in 1862 at Boston, U.S.A. It showed himself and an 'extra' (as the 'spirit' is called) – a transparent, hazy figure of a woman standing by his side. 'This photograph,' he claimed, 'was taken, by myself, on Sunday, when there was not a living soul in the room beside me, so to speak. The form on the right I recognize as my cousin who passed away about twelve years since.' None of this is untrue. The picture had been taken by Mumler himself, and on a Sunday, and with *not a living soul in the room beside himself*. Not even the soul of his dead cousin. Her likeness he had got from an old photo of her, taken when she was alive, and had superimposed it by 'double exposure' (taking two pictures on one negative, the second one of the cousin being under-exposed so that it developed as a hazy, cloudy shape). This technique we often see used now on television. In those days it was unknown, and photography was a strange and almost magic thing. No wonder Mumler's deception went undetected for many months. Then he slipped up. In producing a picture of a spirit relative for one of his clients, the 'ghost' was recognized as a living man Mumler had photographed only a few days before.

Most famous of all these criminals was a Frenchman called Buguet. He was caught and put on trial in April 1875, found guilty, fined heavily, and gaoled for a year. In his studio the police found cardboard dolls, hand-made heads, and all sorts of other bits and pieces Buguet had used to fake his extras. Yet even though he confessed and revealed his methods many of the people he had so callously duped refused to acknowledge he

Dr John Dee (1527–1608), protected by ancient charms, raises a spirit from the dead.
(Radio Times Hulton Picture Library)

Gordon Carroll's ghostly monk. This photo appeared in *The People*, 3 July, 1966. It was taken by an eighteen-year-old clerk, who swore that he was the only person in the church at the time, and that he was amazed, when the film was developed, to see the figure at the altar. (Syndication International)

The Haunted Gallery at Hampton Court Palace. (Department of the Environment)

The so-called Brown Lady of Raynham Hall. The photographer and his assistant who took this photograph found, on developing the picture, a luminous figure whose brilliance seemed to be throwing highlights on to the surrounding woodwork. (Indra Shira)

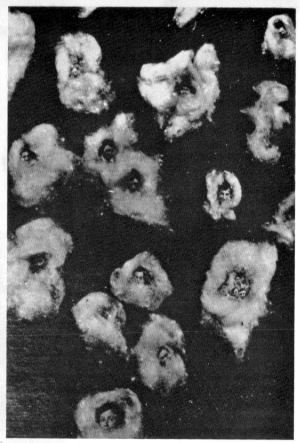

The Falconers' 1925 Armistice Day spirit photograph.
(The Society for Psychical Research)

A group prepared for a table-turning séance. The 'psychic energy' is supposed to be focused through the hands so that the spirit is able to move the table. Table-turning is one of the commonest forms of physical phenomena. (Aldus Books)

The séance room picture was taken by infra-red light on special film. It shows a medium causing a table to levitate. (The Society for Psychical Research)

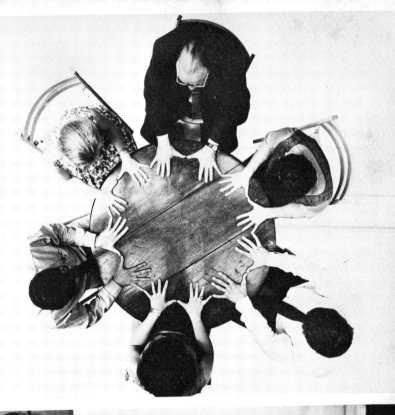

Mrs Rosemary Brown, who is in touch with the composer Franz Liszt, who died in 1886. (Syndication International)

Testing for E.S.P. The man concentrates on one of the five shapes before him while the woman points to the shape she thinks her partner is looking at. A high score might suggest the operation of telepathy. (Duke University Parapsychology Laboratory)

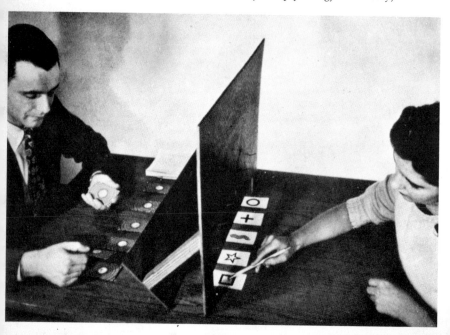

Poltergeists: 8 Court Street, Enniscorthy. There were most mysterious goings-on in the back bedroom of this quiet little house when John Randall went to live there in July 1910. (Billy Quirke)

Exorcism: The casting out of evil spirits, ghosts and such-like phenomena. From earliest times men have tried to rid themselves of unwanted supernatural beings by charms, spells and religious services full of ritual.

a. Maisie Batchelor weeps in the arms of the medium who carried out the exorcism ceremony, with a canon of Southwark Cathedral, London, which finally laid to rest the ghost who had haunted Maisie's house for eighteen years. (Syndication International)

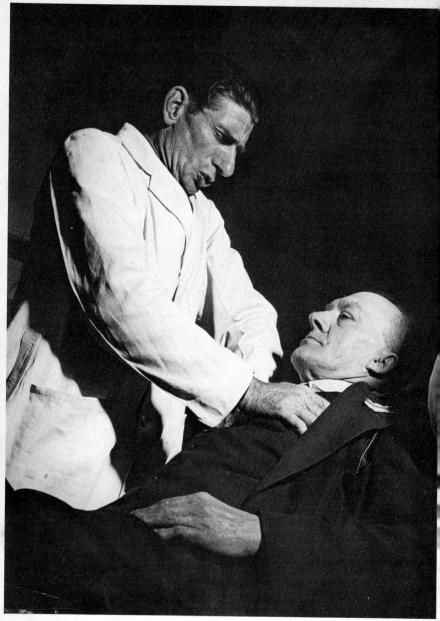

b. Brighton spiritualist, John Thomas, believing himself possessed by the spirit of 'Golden Eagle', a Red Indian doctor who died hundreds of years ago, 'heals' a client by faith, hope and laying on of hands. (Mirror Features)

was guilty and insisted that his photographs of their dead relatives were genuine. There is no limit to human self-deception.

Frederick Hudson, F. M. Parkes, Richard Boursnell, George Moss, John Myers, and, most successful of them all, William Hope, a carpenter of Crewe: these are the most notorious of the British 'spirit photographers'. All of them used the now old-fashioned plate camera and were at work before the 1930s. This apparatus and the process of exposure and development of the sensitive glass plate on which the pictures were taken were crude and simple by today's standards of photographic technology. For this reason it was easy to tamper with the picture, but equally easy for another person with a knowledge of the methods to detect interference. By the middle of the 1930s, when the last of the successful fakers, John Myers, was plying his trade, the situation was changing. The kind of cameras and small-size, factory-prepared-and-processed roll film we are familiar with nowadays were beginning to appear. These are not so easy to meddle with: the photographer must be extremely skilled and very knowledgeable about techniques if he is deliberately to fake a picture and to go on doing so time and again in order to make money. As a result, professional 'spirit' photographers are now rare and looked upon with suspicion.

Anyone who wants to study this aspect of the subject in detail cannot do better than begin by reading *'Spirit' Photography* by Simeon Edmunds, a pamphlet published by the Society for Psychical Research. Its last paragraph sums up the situation:

Every spirit photographer who has been thoroughly and competently investigated has been proved fraudulent. No reliable record appears to exist of a definitely recognized spirit extra being obtained on any photograph under completely fraudproof conditions. Every spirit photograph submitted to expert examination could, in the absence of fraudproof conditions, have been produced, either de-

liberately or accidentally, by normal photographic processes. Therefore, while it cannot be proved that spirit photography is impossible,
there appears to be no real evidence to warrant rational belief in
such a phenomenon.

The pictures which nowadays make the news and cause a ripple
of interest are always of the spontaneous kind, like Gordon
Carroll's and Mr Hardy's. And fascinating, even persuasive
though these may be, it is nevertheless true that such pictures
cannot ever be more than curiosities. They cannot of themselves
be accepted as proof of the existence of ghosts.

8 · Mediums, Séances, and Spiritualism

MEDIUMS: people who claim they have special powers or gifts which enable them to communicate with the 'spirits' of the dead. There are two kinds of medium. A *physical medium* claims that through him the spirits cause objects to float in the air and to appear and disappear, that they tap out messages, and even 'materialize' (take a visible form) so that people can see them. A *mental medium* claims that the spirits take possession of his body and mind so that they can speak aloud and write messages. Some mediums are both physical and mental communicators, while others say that they can only hear what the spirits tell them and are not possessed. (Ordinary people who seem to be gifted with psychic power and 'see' ghosts or feel their presence but do not claim to be a channel of communication between the living and the dead are not called mediums. The proper name for them is 'sensitives'.) Mediums are usually professional, they earn money by conducting *séances* (see below). They have been called the ghosts' earthly colleagues.

SEANCES: the name given to meetings at which two or more people sit round a table or a room and try to summon up the spirits of the dead, usually with the help of a medium (see Plate 6).

SPIRITUALISM: a belief which teaches that people live on after death and that their spirits can and do return to our life in order to contact people through 'mediums' during séances. For followers of the Spiritualist movement ghosts are as real as the man next door. They would never ask, 'Do ghosts exist?' because they believe completely that they do. And their belief is based on what they have seen and heard, felt, and experienced at séances run by those who come nearest to being priests in their church: the mediums.

There have always been 'sensitives'; and witches and witch-doctors and gypsies and wise old women and prophets and saints and even mad people too have all, from time to time, been credited with the gift of 'second sight', or of power over spirits, or have been accused of consorting with ghosts. But only with Spiritualism did there arise the kind of ghost-hunting professional now called a medium. No one genuinely interested in paranormal phenomena can possibly ignore their claims, and so we must look at what has been discovered about them, and the movement that nurtured them.

Spiritualism was started by two young girls, sisters called Kate and Margarette Fox. In 1848 Kate was twelve and Margarette fifteen years old, and they lived with their poverty-stricken parents in a broken-down wooden house in Hydesville, a small village in New York State, U.S.A. Mr Fox was an honest farmer who struggled to bring his family up in decency and as good members of the Methodist chapel.

In normal circumstances the sisters would have lived their humble lives unknown to the world beyond the boundaries of their village, and, as it turned out, might have been the happier for that mundane fate. But it was not to be. During the early weeks of 1848 loud bangs and rappings were heard night and day echoing round the house, noises so loud and so violent that – at least as the story was later told – the place shook to the foundations and the furniture rattled. On 31 March, the disturbance still in full swing, Kate took it into her head to do something others have done before and since in such situations. She spoke to what she supposed was the ghost causing the row and asked it to tell her, by rapping, how many fingers she held open to view. A reply came back at once, and the number of bangs was correct. Nowadays, of course, we would say that a poltergeist was at work and look to Kate and her sister for explanation (see Chapter 11). We would certainly not, or I hope we would not, imagine such a trivial occurrence was reason enough to start a religion. But that is just what happened on this historic day in Hydesville.

The history of Spiritualism, and the faith of hundreds of thousands of its adherents, began with this twelve-year-old girl's playful action. The fact is people were waiting just then for something like Spiritualism to come along and grip them. Only the year before, people all over America had been reading a book called *The Principles of Nature*, which spoke in vivid if not very skilled language about the spirits and how they 'commune with one another while one is in the body and the other is in the higher spheres'. And soon, the book proclaimed, this would be demonstrated. People would hear the spirits of the dead speaking to the people of this world. The book was written by Andrew Davis Jackson of Poughkeepsie, New York State, an apprentice shoemaker and an ignorant youth with little to commend him, who had fallen into the hands of a professional hypnotist who toured the country giving demonstrations of his art. There is no evidence that the Fox family had read Jackson's book. Nevertheless if the sisters can be regarded as the founders of the movement that became Spiritualism then Andrew Davis Jackson was the prophet who went before proclaiming the Spiritualist age to come.

By the end of the day on 31 March the Fox family, astounded by the success of Kate's experiment, had worked out a rough code of raps by which the 'ghost' could answer their questions. What's more, news of this unearthly conversation spread like wild-fire round the village and before long the house was packed with excited neighbours consumed with curiosity and wonder. They remained all night, and a thrilling time they had. One neighbour, a man named Duesler, helped to improve the code of rapped-out replies: one rap would mean yes, two raps would mean no.[1] Using Duesler's method, the 'spirit' now revealed that it was the ghost of a man called Charles Rosma, a pedlar who had been murdered five years before by a Mr and Mrs Bell, who lived in the Fox house at the time. They had wanted his money, had killed him and buried his body in the cellar.

This startling news sent a party of men scurrying down the cellar steps. To their further amazement they heard noises pounding under the floor. Had it not been for the spring floods just then waterlogging the area they would have excavated at once. Instead, they kept their patience until summer, when digging took place. Five feet down their spades turned over some bits of crockery, scraps of charcoal, signs of quicklime, a few strands of hair, and a piece of bone. The bone, said a doctor, *might* have belonged to a human skull.

Here indeed was food for speculation! Maybe the charcoal had been used to burn the pedlar's corpse? And wasn't quick-lime used to decompose flesh and bone? Couldn't the strands of hair have fallen unnoticed from the dead man's head? Wouldn't skull-bone be very difficult to destroy completely? Best of all, weren't these tantalizing remains proof that there really was a spirit haunting the house and that it told the truth? Hydesville was soon in an uproar of controversy, and the villages and towns across the land took up the argument as the days went by and the incredible story got into the newspapers.

At this dramatic moment a young woman named Lucretia Pulver appeared on the scene and told a remarkable story that

1. Later, as Spiritualism developed, Duesler's code was further improved until it became the spiritual morse code now used by mediums.

seemed to support all the ghost had communicated to the world through the Fox sisters. In a sworn statement, Lucretia testified that she had been a servant to the Bells when they lived in the village. One day a pedlar arrived and soon afterwards Mrs Bell sacked Lucretia because she could no longer afford her wages. Before leaving, Lucretia arranged with the pedlar to deliver to her parents' home some of her possessions. The pedlar never arrived, and three days later Mrs Bell hired Lucretia again, much to the girl's surprise. When she returned she noticed that Mrs Bell was making alterations to some men's clothes and that various items were lying about the house which she had last seen in the pedlar's possession. Furthermore, she found that one part of the cellar floor had been disturbed: the earth was soft and uneven. She mentioned this to her mistress who blamed the rats, after which Mr Bell spent a long time in the cellar, saying he was filling up the rat holes.

To many, this seemed ample evidence to prove that Kate and Margarette had found the way through to the Other Side, the Beyond where the spirits of the dead waited for contact from friends and relatives. Before long, conversing with spirits by rapping – and then by other methods too, by automatic writing and speaking while under trance, and finally by 'manifestation' when the ghost appeared in visible form – swept the country in a fashionable craze. Scenes like that at Hydesville on 31 March 1848 were repeated everywhere, and people suddenly discovered powers they had so far spent their lives quite ignorant of, powers which turned them overnight into mediums. The séance had been invented. And when disbelievers said they had tried to contact the Beyond and heard nothing, the believers replied this only went to show that the spirits wanted nothing to do with those who lacked faith.

As for Kate and Margarette, they became national heroines, celebrities as famous and sought-after as pop stars today.

Admirers crowded into Hydesville just to catch a glimpse of them. Life was so difficult that their mother sent them to their married sister, Mrs Fish, who lived in Rochester, a town not far away. If she hoped they would have rest and peace there, she was mistaken. For the ghostly Charles Rosma, not to be left out of things, made the journey as well and began knocking away happily in Mrs Fish's house. Shortly, even she announced that the spirits spoke through her just as they did through her younger sisters. Messages flooded from the three of them to the delight of their followers and the increase of their fame.

Spiritualism had arrived. But there were already those who questioned it. Three professors from the University of Buffalo suggested that, far from being caused by a ghost, the raps were made by the sisters themselves. They had seen a woman who could produce similar noises by moving her knees in such a manner that the bones of the joints dislocated and knocked together. Eventually, Kate and Margarette submitted to a test. They were asked to contact their spirit while sitting with their legs stretched out in front of them and their heels resting on a cushion. In this position the knees and feet were prevented from moving even slightly in the way necessary to cause dislocation noises. Not surprisingly, the sisters found themselves unable to contact their spirit under those conditions. On another occasion Mrs Sidgwick, a psychical investigator, stood Kate on a stool and held her legs firmly. Once again, Kate found it impossible to produce any sounds.

Others began to question the Hydesville events. And they were right to do so, for the evidence given was thin and suspect. Consider the noises in the cellar, for example. The spring floods were at their height and the house was in poor repair. Might not the movement of water under the house have caused the thumping sounds and have shaken the building, vibrating it eerily? And the items dug up from the cellar – how good are they as evidence? Crockery and charcoal are often found under old houses, the hair could have been anyone's, and the only really interesting discovery, the piece of bone, *might* have been human, but was never subjected to tests to *prove* that it was.

Look also at the ghost's story combined with Lucretia's circumstantial confirmation. If what was said was true then Mr and Mrs Bell were murderers. Yet the police took no action against them, even though they were living in New York and publicly denied having killed anyone. Nor was any attempt made to investigate the accusation nor to find the missing Charles Rosma – if anyone of that name ever existed. A not unimportant question that must be asked is: why did Lucretia wait for five years to tell what she knew? And why did she come forward at that precise moment during the Hydesville excitement – a moment trembling with drama and tension? How well did this local girl know the Fox sisters? Well enough to be an accomplice in a deliberate fraud? Or was she a lonely young woman taking an unexpected chance to get into the limelight, to be famous for a happy moment? Or, on the other hand, was she simply an honest citizen trying to do her duty?

We do not know enough about Lucretia Pulver. We do know, however, that in 1888 Kate and Margarette confessed publicly that they had acted fraudulently, and demonstrated how they had produced the noises. They had cracked their toe joints, just as some people crack their knuckles. Later they recanted. But by then the sisters had discredited themselves; and living a lie under the strain of constant publicity broke them down. They comforted themselves with alcohol and ended their extraordinary careers in a pitiful alcoholic haze, no longer capable of separating their own lies from the truth.

Spiritualism got off to a bad start and its development has been chequered ever since. Even so, many thousands of honest, sincere, and intelligent people have found, and still do find, it gives them spiritual peace. And this fact must be set against what I and others think: that these good people are frequently misled and even deliberately deceived by some of those mediums who conduct private séances and the rather dull and unimpressive public services at which hymns are sung and 'messages' delivered to the living from the dead. Most of the followers of Spiritualism are not experts studying psychical phenomena, and cling to their faith because they want very much to be in touch with the after-life. Put together, these two facts suggest why it is that fraud-ulent mediums find it easy to deceive people by tricks so obvious and crude that any stage conjurer would be ashamed to perform them.

For many years the Society for Psychical Research has offered a reward to anyone who can produce physical phenomena under scientifically controlled conditions. The offer presently stands at £1,000, yet no medium has ever come forward to claim it. Artists, scientists of all kinds, engineers, writers, musicians, medical doctors, scholars submit their work to investigation by impartial judges expert in their subject. How strange that people who claim they are in touch with another world beyond our own – a power of considerable importance if their claims are true – are so unwilling to submit themselves to skilled examination. The reason may be that many of the professional mediums since the Fox sisters' time who have either willingly or unwillingly been inspected have been either caught at least once practising fraud, or have been unable satisfactorily to demonstrate their powers.

In a valuable book, *Psychical Research Today*, Dr D. J. West, an expert investigator, describes a typical séance.

I was taken to one recently by someone who, after his wife's death, had become a fervent Spiritualist. He hoped to convert me and get my support for his favourite medium. I was told to be sure not to say who I was as the medium and his friends were suspicious of investigators. The medium had been in practice many years, and

I knew his reputation. The séance was held in pitch darkness in the back parlour of a small private house. The sitters were placed in a circle round the room, the medium among them. Those seated close to the medium were his trusted friends, the 'strong sitters', who were supposed to lend power for the phenomena. No search of the medium or of the room was invited. There was continuous singing during the séance led by a loud-voiced lady who gave us a mixture of popular songs and rousing hymns like 'Onward Christian Soldiers'. The din was horrible, but she kept us at it without pause. There was nothing to stop the medium doing anything he wanted under cover of the noise and darkness.

The materializations would have been invisible but for two small plaques, faintly luminous on one side. Most of the time these plaques were face down in the centre of the floor. When a spirit wanted to show itself, it bent down so as to cast a dim glimmer on its face and body. All that could be seen was an unrecognizable human shape in some white fabric. The shape would go up to one or other of the sitters who would claim to see in it a dead relative. There would be a lull in the singing and the sitter would have a brief conversation with the supposed spirit, usually terminating with a parting kiss. I was not granted such a visitation, but the lady who was with me told me afterwards that the spirit's breath smelt of stale tobacco. One of the spirits was supposed to be a child, and greeted the company in a masculine lisp that was meant for childish prattle but sounded more like something heard on a street corner late at night. The whole performance was so crude that it was amazing that anyone could be taken in by it.

Anyone who has played the party game called 'Ghosts', in which the lights are turned out and someone dressed in a white sheet enters the room with a torch shining dimly on him, knows just how the right atmosphere and gloomy darkness can make your best friend covered in a sheet something to be afraid of. And time and again stage conjurers have demonstrated how sleight of hand, covered by much fast talking and a bit of music, can deceive the eye of watchful spectators, even when the performance takes place in the glare of the spotlight. Not surprisingly, then, people *are* easily taken in and deceived.

Dr West also describes an experience that shows why it is not worth while even exposing fraudulent mediums.

I once tried to expose such a medium. I got into the circle by making friends with some Spiritualists. Among the regular manifestations were spirit hands which travelled round the circle of sitters in the dark, patting knees and shaking hands. I came prepared with some red ink which I smeared over my own hand before the spirit touched me. Sure enough, when the light went on, the medium's hand was smeared. There was an uproar, and I was expelled from the house in disgrace. The sitters' faith in the medium was unshaken, but they suspected that a bad spirit had got into me. They explained that it was the ectoplasm[1] withdrawing into the medium's body that had left behind the stain on her skin.

In other words, as I've said before in this book, when people are determined to believe something, nothing will change their minds, and fighting against their belief may even strengthen it.

But we must be careful. Mediums and Spiritualism may offer little of value in studying ghosts and hauntings, and fraud and deception so often discovered may put us off balance. But we should not be tempted to think that all mediums – or all those who claim a gift of psychic power – are cheats and liars, nor that all séance-produced phenomena are nothing but conjuring tricks. This is not necessarily true. Some of the phenomena, though they may have nothing to do with ghosts as people usually think

1. *Ectoplasm:* A substance that some physical mediums claim their bodies give out during séances. The substance is supposed to form itself into the shape of limbs, faces, and even whole bodies of the spirits who are said to be communicating through the medium. Ectoplasm is very easy to fake – with muslin or other light, misty materials – and many so-called mediums have been caught in acts of fraud using such tricks.

of them, and a lot to do with hallucinations and self-produced apparitions (like the 'experimental' ghost discussed on page 38), are, in themselves, of scientific interest as evidence that might help us explain how the human mind works. Dr West sums it all up like this:

... the possibility that some of the supposed phenomena are hallucinatory shows how unsatisfactory investigation into the alleged phenomena of the séance room has been. Repetition under laboratory conditions is what is needed, but there are no mediums able or willing to give us that. Some investigators say that physical phenomena have so often been proved fraudulent that it is a waste of time to bother with them. Nevertheless, doubt must remain ... Recent laboratory experiments indicate that sometimes the human will can influence the fall of dice. If this is indeed established ... it looks as if physical phenomena of a sort do occur. It is this which makes one hesitate to reject outright all séance room observations.

Now that universities in America and Russia have departments devoted to psychical research, perhaps we shall one day be able to answer the many questions mediums and séances raise. Meanwhile, there is plenty to puzzle, interest, and even amuse us. Like Mrs Rosemary Brown of Wimbledon (see Plate 8). This extraordinary woman says she is in touch with the spirit of the dead composer Franz Liszt, who died in 1886. She is, it seems, on such familiar terms with him that he had dictated music and introduced her to many other famous, dead musicians: Beethoven, Bach, Rachmaninoff, for instance, and quite recently to Igor Stravinsky who died only in 1971. All of these musicians talk to Mrs Brown (Beethoven is 'a slightly crusty old gentleman whose English is improving', she told a *Sunday Times* reporter) and have dictated so many new compositions that she has a vast library of scores. Doctors of music and doctors of the mind have both failed to discover how Mrs Brown does it. Though she can play the piano well enough to perform in public, she has little skill as a composer and cannot simply be hoodwinking everyone. On the contrary, the one thing most of the people who have met her agree upon is that Mrs Brown genuinely believes what she claims is true. She is one of the honest 'mediums', someone who has experiences very difficult to explain away and which we need to learn far more about than we presently know.

PART THREE

Poltergeists

9 · Noise-ghosts

When a place is haunted by an invisible spirit that breaks crockery and moves furniture, rings bells and pulls blankets off beds, bangs doors, taps on table-tops, and throws all manner of objects about, then you know a poltergeist is at work. Mischievous, unpredictable, amusing as well as frightening, poltergeists can come and go suddenly, unexpectedly, and for no obvious reason. They are found in almost every part of the world, and have been known for hundreds, even thousands of years. And they can do almost anything. In some places people have lived happily with them for generations. In other places they have turned normally calm and intelligent folk into nervous wrecks, and succeeded in driving entire families from their homes.

Poltergeists are, I think, the most interesting ghosts of all. Their name is made up of two German words: *polter* meaning 'noise', and *geist* meaning 'spirit' or 'ghost'. But they are capable of far more than simply being noisy ghosts. A list of their activities, recorded in hundreds of cases, is very long. And perhaps their favourite, the way in fact that poltergeist hauntings often begin, is stone-throwing. Astonished witnesses will see pebbles and even small rocks come flying through the air from all sides – and this may happen indoors as well as out in the open. It happened to Andrew Mackie and his family during the famous Scottish haunting that began in February 1695 at Ringcroft Farm, Galloway. More than two hundred years later, on 29 November 1927, the same thing happened to eighty-six-year-old Henry

Robinson and his relatives at their home in Eland Road, Battersea. The police thought Henry's son, Fred, was responsible, but he wasn't. The haunting continued after the police had taken him to hospital for a mental examination.

Throwing stones is only a beginning. Almost any object will do as a missile. In Sid Mularney's garage at Leighton Buzzard in 1963 spanners and hammers and spare motorcycle parts were hurled about as Mr Mularney worked late one night. One hundred and fourteen years earlier in another workshop, this time a carpenter's, at Swanland near Hull, another poltergeist gave the men there a similar, unpleasant time. One of the men, Mr Bristow, told the story and I shall quote his record of what happened because he tells about other things besides 'flying objects':

On the morning when the phenomena took place I was working at the bench next to the wall, where I could see the movements of my two companions and watch the door. Suddenly one of them turned round and called out: 'You had better keep those blocks of wood and stick to work, mates!' We asked him to explain, and he said: 'You know quite well what I mean; one of you hit me with this piece of wood,' and he showed us a piece of wood about an inch square. We both protested that we had not thrown it; and I for one was quite certain my other companion had never stopped working. The incident was being forgotten, when some minutes afterwards, the other companion turned round like the first, and shouted at me: 'It is you, this time, who threw this piece of wood at me!' and he showed me a piece the size of a matchbox. There were two of them accusing me, now, and my denials counted for nothing, so that I laughed and added: 'Since I did not do it, I suppose that if someone was aiming at you it is now my turn.' I had hardly said this when a piece hit me on the hip. I called out: 'I am touched. There is a mystery somewhere; let us see what happens.'

We searched inside and out, but could discover nothing. This strange and embarrassing occurrence gave us much to talk about, but in the end we set to work again.

I had hardly started when some Venetian blinds, held above by beams let into the wall, started shaking with such a clatter that it seemed as if they must be broken to bits. We thought at once, 'Somebody is up there.' I seized a ladder, rushed up and craned my neck, but to find that the blinds were immovable and covered with a layer of dust and cobwebs. As I descended and found myself with my head on a level with the beams, I saw a small piece of wood, two fingers thick, hop forward on a plank, and with a final bound of two feet, pass close to my ear. Dumfounded, I jumped to earth, and then I said: 'This is nothing to laugh at. There is something supernatural. What do you say?' One of my companions agreed with me, the other still maintained that somebody was making fun of us. During this little dispute a bit of wood from the entrance end of the workshop flew and hit him on his hat. I shall never forget the sheepish look on his face.

From time to time a piece of wood, just cut, and fallen upon the floor, jumped up on the benches and started to dance amidst the tools. And it is remarkable that in spite of innumerable attempts, we could never catch a piece in a movement, for it cleverly eluded our stratagems. They seemed animated and intelligent.

I remember a piece which jumped from the bench onto an easel standing three yards away, whence it bounded onto another piece of furniture, then into a corner of the shop, where it stopped. Another traversed the shop like an arrow at the level of three feet above the ground.

Immediately afterwards a piece took flight with a wavy motion. Another went in a slanting line and then alighted quickly at my feet. While the chief of the works, Mr Clarke, was explaining the details of a drawing, and we were both holding our fingers out in such a way that between our fingers there was a distance rather less than an inch, a pointed piece of wood passed between our two fingers and hit the table.

This state of things continued with more or less intensity during six weeks, and always in broad daylight. Sometimes there was comparative quiet for a day or two, during which one or two manifestations occurred, but then followed days of extraordinary activity, as if they wanted to make up for time lost. In one of these periods, while a workman was repairing a Venetian blind shutter on the bench next to mine, I saw a piece of wood about six inches square and one inch thick rise up and describe three-quarters of a large circle in the air and then hit the shutter with some force just at the spot at which the man was working. It was the largest piece of wood which I had seen in the air. Most of them were no larger than an ordinary box of matches, though they were of various shapes, the last flying piece that I saw was of oak and about 2½ inches square and one inch thick. It fell on me from the far corner of the ceiling, and described in its course a screw line like a spiral staircase of about twenty inches diameter. It is necessary to add that all these objects, without exception, came from the interior of the shop, and that none came in by the door.

One of the strangest peculiarities of the manifestations consisted in this, that the pieces of wood cut by us and fallen on the ground worked their way into the corners of the shop, from where they raised themselves to the ceiling in some mysterious and invisible manner. None of the workmen, none of the visitors, who flocked here in great numbers during the six weeks of these manifestations, ever saw a single piece in the act of rising. And yet the pieces of wood, in spite of our vigilance, quickly found their way up in order to fall on us where nothing existed a moment before. By degrees we got used to the thing, and the movements of the pieces of wood, which seemed to be alive and some cases even intelligent, no longer surprised us and hardly attracted our attention . . .

Except in some special cases, the projectiles fell and hit without any noise, although they came at such a speed that in normal conditions they would have produced a fairly loud clatter.

Mr Bristow's story can be read in full in Volume VII of the *Proceedings* of the Society for Psychical Research, where it first appeared after Mr Bristow had been closely questioned by one of the Society's experts, Mr Myers. Some of the details noticed during the Swanland haunting are typical of many poltergeist incidents. As, for example, the weird feeling Mr Bristow had that the pieces of wood were 'animated and intelligent', that they were 'alive'. In other words, he felt that what was happening was not accidental and haphazard, but directed by someone – by a person. It is this feeling, experienced by many witnesses of poltergeist activity, which makes this kind of haunting so frightening. If something happens accidentally – like a vase slipping off a rickety shelf or a door blowing shut – we do not feel afraid. Somehow we know the occurrence was not deliberately caused. But if our hairbrush rises into the air before our very eyes, and flies at us in a way it could never do by accident, and *no one is present who could have thrown it* ...? Then we feel afraid – there is no obvious, natural explanation for what happened.

What is more, this feeling that the flying objects are being 'guided' is strengthened by the fact that they often follow flight paths they could not possibly follow in ordinary, natural conditions, *even if they had been thrown*. Sometimes they curve round corners, sometimes they twist about in the air. Mr Bristow saw a piece of wood travel 'with a wavy motion. Another went in a slanting line', whilst the last piece he saw during the haunting 'described in its course a screw line like a spiral staircase of about twenty inches diameter'. Only a few years ago, the proprietor of the Garrick's Head Hotel, Bath, witnessed his own cash-register lift from the counter in the bar, move forward a few feet – all quite deliberately – and then crash down to the floor, breaking a chair as it fell.

Stranger still, considering how dangerous it is to be in a room where guided missiles fly about in all directions, very few people have ever been hurt by them. To start with, the objects usually seem to avoid hitting witnesses. It is as though the poltergeists wanted to frighten but not to hurt onlookers. And even when people have been struck, they have frequently noted, with surprise, how soft the blow was, and how little damage was done to them physically. Mr Bristow mentions pieces of wood falling on himself and his colleagues many times, but not once does he report harm done. Sid Mularney survived an attack by spanners, hammers, and numerous nuts and bolts without one bruise to show for it. Andrew Mackie, it is true, was beaten from his house by wooden sticks laid about him by invisible hands, and Esther Cox, during the haunting known as the Great Amherst Mystery, was struck and injured more than once. But these are rare cases, the exceptions that prove the rule.

Not only do poltergeists make objects fly, they also make them land without bouncing or rolling, a feature that deepens the impression that they are under the control of an intelligent being. Almost anything hurled across a room will skid about when it lands, or bounce or roll; only something placed down will stay still. And though, as Mr Bristow records from his own experience, objects propelled by poltergeists seem to avoid being caught while in flight (Mr Bristow says, 'we could never catch a piece in movement, for it cleverly eluded our stratagems'), when they come to rest and are picked up many witnesses have been surprised to find that the objects are warm, and even at times too hot to hold.

Playing with fire is, in fact, one of the most dangerous and horrifying of all the 'tricks' poltergeists get up to. The Robinsons of Eland Road, Battersea, discovered this. On one occasion, their washerwoman came to Fred Robinson 'in a state of terror and pointed to a heap of red-hot cinders in the outhouse. There was no fire near. How could they have got there?' During the great Amherst haunting in 1879, lighted matches, it is claimed, fell from the ceiling, clothes locked in cupboards burst into flames, and finally (as a ghostly voice had foretold!) the house itself was burnt down. Borley Rectory in Suffolk, scene of so many hauntings it was called the most haunted house in Britain, burnt to the ground mysteriously on the night of 27–28 February 1939, an event some people blame on the rectory's famous poltergeist.

These are just some of the commonest features to be found in poltergeist activities; there are many more which happen less often. As, for example, their ability to move objects and even animals into places where they would not ordinarily be found. A cow was discovered in a hayloft when Birchen Bower farm at Hollinwood in Lancashire was being haunted. There was no way the animal could have got up there by itself and the only way it could be got down again was by winching it out with a block and tackle through a loading door in the wall. Sometimes poltergeists will 'talk' by tapping in reply to question asked by witnesses. Sir William Barrett, who investigated the Enniscorthy Case (see page 116), once asked a poltergeist to tap out the number of fingers he had spread open. The spirit always gave the correct number of taps, even though Sir William kept his hand in his pocket where it could not be seen by anyone who might have been playing a hoax. Others have conducted similar experiments, with equally puzzling results. This 'trick' is also used, of course, in séances when mediums pretend to get in touch with the souls of the dead. The spirits are asked to tap 'one for yes and two for no' in answer to the medium's questions. Unfortunately, such tapped out replies are very easy to fake and many gullible people have been taken in by confidence tricksters (see Chapter 8).

Some poltergeists have shown enormous strength. The one in Sid Mularney's garage appears to have thrown heavy motorcycles about the place. Many people, including Andrew Mackie and eighteen-year-old John Randall, whose story is told in Chapter 11, have been lifted or dragged from their beds. In a number of accounts, the shifting of awkward and heavy bits of furniture is noted. In the haunting called the T. B. Clarke Case, a huge cupboard which stood on a landing was seen descending the stairs, carefully turning the corner between each flight. There are even a few stories in which it is claimed that not only objects but living people were transported through the air from one place to another, sometimes a great distance away.

We just don't yet know enough about this fascinating phenomenon. We do not yet know enough ... This is the answer we have to give to so many of the questions that come to mind when we think about ghosts. For the most part, we can only make intelligent guesses. So what are the guesses we can make about poltergeists? What are they? How are they caused? Why do they behave as they do? Even the simplest answers are complicated and difficult to sort out clearly. Nevertheless, I have tried in Chapter 11 to suggest a theory that interests me. Before then, however, let's look at the solutions people found years ago, and then at a well-documented and typical poltergeist haunting, the Enniscorthy Case.

10 · Witches, Ghosts, and Bogles

Magic spells cast by evil witches were believed, years ago, to be one of the causes of what we today would call poltergeist activity. It was a belief that led to ugly scenes: to witch hunts, and witch trials, and even to the unfortunate victims being tortured and cruelly put to death.

In 1582, for example, at St Osyth near Clacton-on-Sea, Essex, at least thirteen women (it could have been as many as eighteen or nineteen – the records are not clear on the number) were tried and executed because they were thought to be witches who caused unnatural disturbances. A century later, in 1692, at Salem near Boston, U.S.A., a pious community of Puritan settlers put on trial several women as well as the Reverend George Burroughs, accusing them of causing poltergeist hauntings. This notorious affair came as the climax of a long series of events which began at Newberry in 1679. In that year William Morse heard 'a noise upon the roof of the house, as if sticks and stones had been thrown against it with great violence'. Soon his home was in chaos with furniture scattered everywhere. And in the next few days worse was to happen, for his small son was 'flung about in such a manner as that they feared his brains would have been beaten out'. When he was put to bed, the bed itself leaped up and down, the clothes were flung off it, and there was no peace till he got up. After that, the boy was pinched, beaten, thrown into the fire, and – oddest manifestation of all – started barking like a dog and clucking like a hen and was quite unable to control himself. Nicholas Desborough of Hartford, Connecticut, fared little better in 1682. He was 'strangely molested by stones, pieces of earth, and cobs of Indian corn ... There was no great violence in the motion, though several persons of the family, and others also, were struck with the things that were thrown by an invisible hand, yet they were not hurt thereby.'

After a long series of fearful events such as these, all of them at that time inexplicable and mysterious, a community of people can become so frightened that they look round desperately for some cause, any cause, they can understand and blame, can deal with and so rid themselves of their fear. Believing in magic and in witches, as people did then, it was easy to fix the responsibility for the hauntings on anyone who was suspected of witchcraft. So it was at Salem.

Nowadays, no one really believes that poltergeists are the work of witches' spells, even though at Hallowe'en we remember the night in the year when, according to tradition, witches meet and make powerful magic. Not that our parties and jokes and celebrations are anything like what used to happen in the days when people performed certain rituals to protect themselves on the 'witching night'. And those days are not so very long ago; there are old people living who can remember them from their childhood. I recently came across an account by one of them in *More Tales from the Fens* by W. H. Barrett, and it is so interesting, because of the details it tells us about the way people used to behave, that I cannot resist quoting some of it here:

I reckon I was a lad of about seven or eight when ... I was sent to stay with an old aunt in one of the loneliest parts of the Fens. She had a big family, this aunt, though most of them were grown up by then, except for a boy of fifteen and a girl of twelve.

Although there wasn't another house within a mile, that didn't bother them; the farm was run by the family, and for most of the year they went to bed when it got dark and got up at daybreak.

While I was there Hallowe'en came round [31 October]. In the afternoon everyone was busy putting osier twigs [osier is a kind of willow] in front of all the doors and windows, the pigsties, stables and cow-house.

Uncle killed one of his black hens and hung it on the chicken-house door after he'd pulled out two of its wing feathers and tied them on the yard-dog's collar; then he caught the cats and shut them up in the barn.[1] From all the talk going on, I found out that this was the night when the witches went round the fen, meeting each other and then, at the chiming of midnight, coming to some spot they'd chosen and casting spells over all the folks and animals nearby. That was why the peeled osier rods were put at all the ways into the house because no witch dared cross over them, neither would they go near black chicken feathers.

As the evening went by we all sat round the big open hearth. Aunt didn't put peat on the fire that night because witches could smell peat smoke for miles away, she said; instead, huge logs of oak were blazing away. The candles had been blown out, so the only light we had came from the fire, as we sat and listened to Aunt's stories of what witches could get up to. After supper a plate of thick slices of ham and half a loaf of bread were stood outside on the door-stone so that, if a witch called, she wouldn't have to go away hungry because, if she did, she might start casting her spells on us. Then I was given a glass of ginger wine while my aunt and uncle and the others drank a lot of home-made botanic beer. After a while Uncle stood up and said to me:

'Come along, it's time we were up and doing.'

He told me it was the custom, this night, for the oldest man and the youngest boy in the house to go round the farm an hour before midnight; so we set off. It was very queer padding along behind Uncle as he carried the lantern. All the animals seemed restless, and Uncle said they were like that because they could see and hear things that we couldn't, and they all knew what was going on.

1. The cats were shut away because witches were believed to turn cats especially of all animals into spirits, called 'familiars', which helped the witches make their spells.

Poltergeists

After we'd been round the farmyard we had to visit the bees. As we went into the orchard an owl swooped over us with a loud screech, just above Uncle's head. I was scared, but Uncle got a firm grip of the thick stick he was carrying and, when the owl turned to fly over us again, he caught it such a clout that it fell down to the ground, fluttered its wings a bit and then lay still. My uncle bent down, turned it over and said:

'Well, there's one old witch who won't go home tonight.'

When we got to the bee-hive, we went close up and listened to the noise going on inside; it was just like the hum of a threshing machine on a frosty morning.

'Bor,' said Uncle, 'they're all worked up because they're a lot wiser than we are'; then, after tapping the hive with his stick, he bent right down to the entrance and said:

'Well done, my old beauties. I got one just now and, by the sound of it, you've got another; push her outside when you've done with her.'

When we were back indoors we all sat round the fire again while Uncle told my aunt and the others what had happened while we were out.

'It looks as though some of us will be tudded [bewitched] for sure before morning,' said Aunt, 'if we're not careful. There's nothing, after all, to stop one of those old witches coming down the chimney and casting a spell on us.'

I saw everyone backing away from the fire, and I did so too. Then Aunt got up, went over to the cupboard in the corner and came back with a big brown-paper bag.

'Whatever any old hag turns herself into,' she said, 'I promise I'll make her cough before she gets to the hearth. This ought to make her sneeze a bit first,' and she took a handful of flowers of sulphur out of the bag and threw them on the fire. Bright blue flames and yellow smoke roared up the chimney. Aunt did this several times, even though Uncle told her not to forget that the roof was thatched, and if we were burnt out it wasn't going to be any good blaming it on any witches; but she only told him to be quiet, she knew what she was doing. This started a lot of arguing; everybody joining in till it seemed to me that the witches had been forgotten and that I was in the middle of a good old family row. Anyway, Aunt got into such a temper that she threw the whole bag onto the fire and the yellow smoke came pouring into the room worse than ever, making us all splutter and choke.

Uncle said that two could play at that game and he went over to the cupboard and fetched out a linen bag full of the black gunpowder he used in his muzzle-loader. He'd no sooner hurled it at the back of the fire than there was a hell of a bang and we were all smothered in soot from head to foot. Well, that cleared everybody's temper and when the smoke had cleared away a bit Uncle said: 'Well, I'll be damned,' because lying on Aunt's lap was a jackdaw just kicking out his last gasp. And just then the old grandfather clock struck midnight.

After that we all ate a lot of thick ham sandwiches and the others drank some more botanic beer and I had another glass of ginger wine. Then Uncle said to me: 'Come on, bor. We've got to make another round.'

It was still very dark when we got outside, but all the animals were quiet and settled down. When we got to the orchard we found the bees quiet, too, but on the flight board, believe it or not, was a dead mouse, still warm. Uncle picked it up then went back to fetch the owl he'd killed the time we went out before. When we were back in the house he threw the owl, the mouse and the jackdaw on the fire and said:

'Three witches on one Hallowe'en isn't a bad bag. Now, all of you get to bed and sleep well. You won't have to worry about any witches for another twelvemonth.'

Apart from its interest as a record of old customs, this is a very good description of how people can turn perfectly ordinary happenings into something odd, mysterious, even frightening. The boy's aunt and uncle had been brought up to believe that witches were dangerous and that they met on Hallowe'en to perform spells, turn themselves into animals, and 'make' ghosts. People therefore had to protect themselves by 'good' magic – customs handed down from father to son and mother to daughter, such as putting osier twigs round doors and windows, locking the cats away, attaching black hen's feathers to the dogs, and laying food on the doorstep to keep any passing witch in a happy mood so that she wouldn't put a spell on the family.

All these things, and others, the farmer and his wife did without question, never stopping for a moment to wonder whether the things they were doing made sense, had any truth or reason in them. And because they were *expecting* certain things to happen, they almost made them happen by the way they behaved. Look, for example, at these events:

1. All the family, we're told, drank a lot of home-made beer that night. They seem to have drunk so much in fact that they began to act foolishly, as drunken people do. The aunt threw flowers of sulphur on the fire thus endangering her home. The uncle, not to be outdone by his wife, and despite his warning, actually throws gunpowder on the flames, causing an explosion which could easily have blown them all to pieces. Would these two usually sensible farming people have acted so stupidly if they had been sober? And would they have done what they did unless they believed they were protecting themselves from witches?

2. The exploding gunpowder killed a jackdaw. The bird was by some fluke sucked down the chimney and landed in the aunt's lap. (Or did it come down the chimney? Was it not perhaps already in the house, lodged in the thatch of the roof? We don't know – *but neither did the people present at the time.*) Everyone believed it was a witch in disguise. But then, as with the owl, would anyone have thought this, had it not been Hallowe'en? Wouldn't they just have dismissed it as an odd accident? On any other night, too, the farmer would have thought nothing of seeing an owl swoop towards him in the dark. It happens often. I've

been swooped at by an owl more than once on a country lane near where I used to live. Certainly, no farmer would normally kill an owl: they are birds of prey that eat mice, rats, and other vermin a farmer wants to be rid of. Only on Hallowe'en would he have acted as he did.

3. The business with the bees and the mouse they kill is just the same: an ordinary event turned into something ominous just because the farmer believed that on this night of the year witches went abroad in the guise of animals. All kinds of things can make bees buzz noisily: a coming thunderstorm, an unexpected find of nectar or pollen, an invader (like a wasp or even a mouse) in the hive, or something bumping against the hive, such as a stray cow, or a badger on the hunt for honey (which they love). Why should the noise the farmer hears be caused by witches? What evidence, other than superstition, has anyone for supposing this is the cause?

4. As for the farm animals which 'seemed restless': the uncle was right, 'they all knew what was going on'! Any farmer will tell you that unusual goings-on upset animals. Even city people who own pets know this: if you have a cat or a dog you'll have seen how uneasy it gets if the family are behaving in an unusual way – preparing to go on a long journey, for example. On Hallowe'en day, the farm animals 'felt' the excitement among the humans. And there was quite enough going on around them to make them restless until well into the night. The pigs and horses and cows had to put up with the commotion of osier twigs being nailed round the doors and windows of the pigsties, the stables and the cowbyres. The hens had to witness one of their number being slaughtered and then hung up, half plucked of its feathers, from the hen-house door. The cats were locked away for the night, which free-roaming cats dislike, and the dogs had to put up with feathers on their collars, which understandably annoyed them. The unease the animals felt that night had

nothing to do with witches, and everything to do with strange behaviour by ordinary people.

5. A last point: anyone who has sat in the dark listening to ghost stories knows how soon he is ready to believe that every sound, every shadow, every movement is a ghost come to haunt him. Some people can get so frightened at such times that they hardly dare move and won't go to bed alone. In fact, given the right conditions, people can be made to believe anything for a short time at least. And all the right conditions were present in the farmhouse that night to make everyone present see witches in the smallest event. A day of excited preparations was followed by an evening when: 'The candles had been blown out, so the only light we had came from the fire, as we listened to Aunt's stories of what witches could get up to.' Harrowing, terrifying stories I'll bet they were too. After them, a dead jackdaw falling down the chimney would seem like the devil himself.

What was Hallowe'en all about? Simply this: In days gone by people were afraid of witches. Once a year, on Hallowe'en night, they gave way to their fear and tried to get rid of it. They 'worked themselves up' into a state of excitement that prepared them to do things they would, in calmer moments, be unable to do. They acted out 'good' magic. And then they spent the evening 'catching' witches-in-disguise. Because the witches-in-disguise were killed there was no longer anything to fear. After that, as the Uncle says, 'You don't have to worry about witches for another twelvemonth.' Everyone felt safe, free from fear, and could 'get to bed and sleep well'.

In the same way, if people thought they were being haunted by a ghost, and believed that the ghost was caused by a witch's spell, then they worked themselves up to get rid of the witch by trial and execution, just as they did at Salem in 1692.

So witches were one explanation people used to give for poltergeists. Another was that they were ghosts – either evil spirits sent by the devil, or the returned souls of dead people. The Reverend Samuel Wesley thought this. He was the father of the famous John Wesley, founder of the Methodist Church, and the Wesley home, Epworth Parsonage, was haunted by a poltergeist for a couple of months in 1716. Mr Wesley thought a devil-spirit was visiting him. One night the poltergeist was knocking on the headboard of the bed where Hetty Wesley, then in her early teens, was sleeping. 'Thou deaf and dumb devil,' Mr Wesley roared at it in anger, 'why dost thou frighten these children...?' In fact, the children were frightened only for a short time. They grew so used to the poltergeist that they called it 'Old Jeffrey' and would send their youngest sister, then no more than a toddler, chasing round the house after it.

There are people even today who think that poltergeists are evil spirits or souls come back from the dead. (I do not agree; but what I do think must wait until the next chapter to be told.)

Witches, ghosts, and now bogles. Bogles are (if you believe in them) mischievous, rather bad-tempered creatures, neither man nor animal. They belong, in fact, to 'the little people' who possess strange powers and are not at all to be trusted. Bogles enjoy performing all the tricks exhibited by poltergeists – stone-throwing, causing chaos with furniture, ringing bells at the wrong time, setting fire to buildings, and so on. And people used to think they, along with witches and ghosts, were the cause of poltergeist hauntings.

The easiest way to appreciate what bogles are supposed to be is to read one of the many old folk tales about them. My favourite, probably because I was born and spent my childhood in the area where it is set, is the story of the bogle at Hilton Castle, County Durham.

113

THE CAULD LAD OF HILTON

in the version told by Joseph Jacobs

At Hilton Hall, long years ago, there lived a Brownie that was the contrariest Brownie you ever knew. At night, after the servants had gone to bed, it would turn everything topsy-turvy, put sugar in the salt cellars, pepper into the beer, and was up to all kinds of pranks. It would throw the chairs down, put tables on their backs, rake out fires, and do as much mischief as could be. But sometimes it would be in a good temper, and then! – 'What's a Brownie?' you say. Oh, it's a kind of a sort of a Bogle, but it isn't so cruel as a Redcap! What! you don't know what's a Bogle or a Redcap! Ah, me! what's the world a-coming to? Of course, a Brownie is a funny little thing, half man, half goblin, with pointed ears and hairy hide. When you bury treasure, you scatter over it blood drops of a newly slain kid or lamb, or better still, bury the animal with the treasure, and a Brownie will watch over it for you, and frighten everybody else away.

Where was I? Well, as I was a-saying, the Brownie at Hilton Hall would play at mischief, but if the servants laid out for it a bowl of cream, or a knuckle cake spread with honey, it would clear away things for them, and make everything tidy in the kitchen. One night, however, when the servants had stopped up late, they heard a noise in the kitchen, and, peeping in, saw the Brownie swinging to and fro on the Jack chain, and saying:

> 'Woe's me! woe's me!
> The acorn's not yet
> Fallen from the tree,
> That's to grow the wood,
> That's to make the cradle,
> That's to rock the bairn,
> That's to grow to the man,
> That's to lay me.
> Woe's me! Woe's me!'

So they took pity on the poor Brownie, and asked the nearest hen-wife what they should do to send it away. 'That's easy enough,' said the hen-wife, and told them that a Brownie that's paid for it's service, in aught that's not perishable, goes away at once. So they made a cloak of Lincoln green, with a hood to it, and put it by the hearth and watched. They saw the Brownie come up, and seeing the hood and cloak, put them on and frisk about, dancing on one leg and saying:

> *'I've taken your cloak, I've taken your hood;*
> *The Cauld Lad of Hilton will do no more good.'*

And with that it vanished, and was never seen or heard of afterwards.

Nor, I think, has anyone anywhere ever seen a bogle of any kind since. But poltergeists still haunt people from time to time.

11 · The Enniscorthy Case . . . and a Theory

John Randall was eighteen years old in July 1910 when his work as a carpenter took him to Enniscorthy, a town in County Wexford, Ireland (see Plate 10). Before he had been there a week he found himself at the centre of a poltergeist haunting which by now has become a classic of its kind.

How do we know what went on in the back bedroom of 8 Court Street where John lodged with two other young men? I am often asked by readers of my other ghost books how information about psychical phenomena comes to light. Well, the Enniscorthy story is typical of many. At the time of the disturbance, there were six people in the house. A labourer called Nicholas Redmond, his wife, three lodgers – John Randall, George Sinnott, also a carpenter, and Richard Roche – and a servant girl called Bridget Thorpe. We can be fairly sure that news of the haunting first got out because at least one of the these six people could not resist telling friends or neighbours about it. Whether this is how they started or not, rumours were very soon spreading round the town about the mysterious goings-on in Court Street. And as is the way with rumours, they eventually reached the offices of the local newspaper, the *Enniscorthy Guardian*.

Newspaper editors like nothing better than a good ghost story: it pleases the readers, fills the columns of papers with mystery and excitement, and helps sell copies. And so a reporter, Mr N. J. Murphy, was instructed to call at the Redmond house and dig out the story. He did a thorough job. Somehow, he persuaded everyone involved to allow him to spend a night in the haunted bedroom in the hope that he might witness with his own eyes what so far only rumour had told him about. This he did on 19 July 1910, accompanied by a friend, Mr Owen Devereux, who kept a bicycle shop in town. The two observers had an unexpectedly rewarding time, and Mr Murphy was so impressed that he not only wrote his story for the local newspaper but contacted Sir William Barrett as well.

Sir William we have come across before. He is the person who experimented with a poltergeist, asking it to tap out the number of fingers he had stretched out in his pocket (see page 103). He was an eminent scientist, a Fellow of the Royal Society, and an expert ghost investigator. He visited Enniscorthy, talked to everyone concerned in the affair, and instructed the important witnesses to record in writing their observations and experiences. This was done by John Randall – the key figure in the case – by Mr Murphy, and by the servant girl Bridget Thorpe. Mr Devereux added a statement confirming the accuracy of Mr Murphy's account, and the Rev. Canon Rennison of Wexford wrote a letter saying he had known John Randall for five years and believed him to be 'a thoroughly truthful and trustworthy boy' whose word could be relied upon.

All these documents were then published in Volume XXV of the *Proceedings* of the Society for Psychical Research. Many reports of ghostly disturbances have come to public attention in this way; and it is from the *Proceedings* that I quote:

STATEMENT WRITTEN BY JOHN RANDALL

On Saturday, the 2nd of July, 1910, I came to work in Enniscorthy as an improver in the carpentry trade. Monday, I went to lodge in a house in Court Street. There were two other men stopping in the same house as lodgers. They slept in the same room also, but shared a different bed at the other side of the room. My bed was in a recess in the wall at the opposite side. There was one large window in the room, which opened both top and bottom. The room was about 14 feet square and 10 feet high. There was one door opening into it. The window described was in the back wall of the house nearly opposite the door opening into the room from the top landing. There were two other doors on the same landing opening into different rooms. There was also a fireplace in the room.

On Monday night, July 4th, we went to bed, and my first night in the strange house I think I slept pretty soundly. We got up at six o'clock the next morning and went to work. We left off work at six in the evening, and went to bed the same time as the night before, between 10 and 10.30 o'clock, slept soundly, and all went well, also on Wednesday.

Went to bed on Thursday night at 10.45, the three of us going as before. We blew out the light, but the room was then fairly lightsome. We had been only about ten minutes in bed when I felt the clothes being drawn gently from my bed. I first thought it was the others that were playing a joke, so I called out, 'Stop, George, it's too cold.' (George being one of their names and the other Richard.) Then I heard them say, 'It's Nick' (that is the name of the man of the house). It wasn't any of them that had pulled the clothes off me, so they thought it was Nick that was in the room, and did not mind.

At this time the clothes had gone off my bed completely, and I shouted to them to strike a match. When they struck a match, I found my bedclothes were at the window. The most curious part was that the same time when the clothes were leaving my bed, their bed was moving. I brought back the clothes and got into bed again. The light was then put out, and it wasn't long until we heard some hammering in the room — tap-tap-tap-like. This lasted for a few minutes, getting quicker and quicker. When it got very quick their bed started to move out across the floor, and that made us very frightened, and what made us more frightened was the door being shut, and nobody could open it without making a great noise.

They then struck a match and got a lamp. We searched the room thoroughly, and could find nobody. Nobody had come in the door.

We called the man of the house (Redmond); he came into the room, saw the bed, and told us to push it back and get into bed (he thought all the time one of us was playing a trick on the other). I said I wouldn't stay in the other bed by myself, so I got in with the others; we put out the light again, and it had been only a couple of minutes out when the bed ran out on the floor with the three of us. Richard struck a match again, and this time we all got up and put on our clothes; we had got a terrible fright and couldn't stick it any longer. We told the man of the house we would sit up in the room until daylight. During the time we were sitting in the room we could hear footsteps leaving the kitchen [which was immediately below the boys' bedroom] and coming up the stairs; it would stop on the landing outside the door and wouldn't come into the room. The footsteps and noises continued through the house until daybreak. We got up at nine o'clock and went to work for a three-quarter day.

That night (Friday) when we went to bed about eleven o'clock we felt a bit nervous in going. We put out the light, and in a few minutes the footsteps started again, and noises. There were also noises like chips being chopped in the kitchen. This night passed over not near so bad as the night before, but yet we were afraid to go to sleep.

Saturday we all went home for the Sunday, but returned Sunday evening. We went to bed Sunday night, as before, and it passed over with very slight noises. On Monday night the noises started again after going to bed, and after about a quarter of an hour their bed ran again. They then struck a light and I got into the bed with them. There were terrible noises everywhere; on the walls, out on the landing, and downstairs. We left the light lighted for some time, and whilst it was lighted, what added more to our fright was a chair dancing out to the middle of the floor without a thing near it. We put out the light again after moving back the bed. Immediately the light was put out the bed ran again out on the floor. Richard had the matches always ready to strike. Every time we would hear a noise and feel the bed moving, we would shout: 'Strike, Richard, strike; we're going again!' We were trembling from head to feet with fear. We left the light lighted till morning after that.

Tuesday night passed over about the same, and on Wednesday

night there wasn't a stir. After hearing nothing on Wednesday night we thought it had stopped, but still we felt nervous. On Thursday night it started as bad as the first night, and several people remarked it being so bad on the night exactly a week after it had started. The bed ran out several times, and what never happened to any one of us before, George was lifted out of bed without a hand near him. He went home next day, and stopped at home for two days. So while he was away, Richard and I stopped in the room. The same noise still continued, and the bed ran also. We went home on Saturday as on the week before.

George came back again on Sunday night, and slept in the same bed with us again, and it wasn't extra bad that night. It went on about the same way every night until the following Friday night, when it was very bad. The bed turned up on one side, and threw us out on the floor, and before we were thrown out, the pillow was taken from under my head three times. When the bed rose up, it fell back without making any noise. This bed was so heavy, it took both the woman and girl to pull it out from the wall without anybody in it, and there was only three castors on it. After being thrown out of the big bed, the three of us got into my bed. We were not long in it when it started to rise, but could not get out of the recess it was in unless it was taken to pieces. It ceased about daybreak, and that finished that night's performance.

It kept very bad then for a few nights. So Mr Murphy, from the *Guardian* office, and another man named Devereux, came and stopped in the room one night. They sat on two chairs in the room, while we [he means himself and George – Richard had left the house by this time] lay each in our own beds. We were not long in bed when I felt a terrible feeling over me like a big weight. I then felt myself being taken from the bed, but could feel no hands, nor could I resist going. All I could say was: 'I'm going, I'm going; they're at me!' I lay on the floor in a terrible state, and hardly able to speak. The perspiration was pouring through me. They put me back in bed again, and nothing more than strange knockings and noises happened between that and morning. We slept again in the room the next night, but nothing serious happened. We then got another lodging, and the people [the Redmonds and Bridget Thorpe] left it also. For the three weeks I was in the house I lost nearly three-quarters of a stone weight. I never believed in ghosts until that, and I think it would convince the bravest man in Ireland.

John William Randall
18 Main St., Enniscorthy

John Randall, Sid Mularney, the Swanland carpenters, Andrew Mackie: they span nearly four hundred years of poltergeist activity. What is the explanation? As I've had to say before, we do not know for certain. There could be more than one solution. And there could be natural as well as supernatural causes. But, for now, I want to do some supposing – some guessing based on a little hard evidence.

Every day we witness the effects of physical energy. We move about, exert our strength to lift objects, walk, kick footballs, throw things, shout, do all manner of activities that require the use of energy. We also witness the effects of concentrated power when it finds an outlet. Under the surface of the earth is locked an enormously powerful force. And it sometimes breaks out, erupting in earthquakes and volcanoes. When this happens, any-thing in the way gets hurled about – rocks, buildings, people. Or think of an explosion of dynamite: locked-in energy suddenly released. Its blast can travel through the air *invisibly* and knock people down, even killing them with the blow.

Now, I think people are like the physical world. They have surprisingly powerful forces locked inside them. Not physical forces only, but mental and emotional ones. Normally, these are deliberately (we say consciously) channelled, like electricity from a generator, into useful activities. We decide to run the mile in four minutes, perhaps, or to climb a mountain – or write a book! We work and play, and thus these powers are used up.

Sometimes, however, this energy gets dammed up inside us. Then we become ill, or we find ourselves behaving strangely or

121

even anti-socially (we might smash things up or attack people or drive a car recklessly). And I think something else also might happen. These mental–emotional powers explode, like an earthquake or volcanic eruption, breaking out from us, and relieving us of the tension they caused when pent up inside. With one difference from the earthquake: there is a human mind directing the explosion. So the forces do not simply spread out in all directions, 'hitting', so to speak, anyone who happens to get in the way. Instead, they are channelled in certain ways. But not deliberately, not consciously. We do it now *unconsciously*. (This is why the people responsible for causing poltergeist upsets do not realize they are the cause, and blame a ghost or something magical.)

Can such mental–emotional action cause chairs to dance across a room, or lift a heavy bed, or pull bedclothes off someone, or throw pieces of wood across a workshop? We know that TELEKINESIS, mind over matter, is something experiments have shown to be possible. But why should anyone, consciously or unconsciously, do anything so childish and apparently point-

---

TELEKINESIS

When ordinary solid objects – cups, chairs, books – and also animals and even people are moved from one spot to another by unknown and invisible forces we call this telekinesis. *The word literally means 'movement at a distance', and it might be described as the power of mind over matter. Experiments have shown that some people, by concentrating strongly enough, can move objects by 'psychic' or, in other words, mental energy alone.*

---

less as the things poltergeists do? To ask that question is like asking why some people deliberately break street lamps, or hack up railway carriage seats, or smash telephone kiosks, or any of the other daft things people do of that kind. The answers are many, but they include the fact that people do such things when they are feeling spiteful, or bitter, or are venting their hatred, or are lonely and unwanted, or feel guilty about something and are trying to cover it up.

I once heard a famous writer tell how, as a teenager, he was very shy of girls. He did not know how to tell a particular girl that he liked her. She would walk past his house and he would look at her and think how attractive she was, and wish desperately he dared ask her to go out with him. But he was shy and couldn't even open his mouth and say hello. So he did something else, something that might to some people seem very odd indeed. He threw stones at her and shouted rude things! It was the only way he could show his feelings – by pretending to be big, tough, couldn't-care-less. When all the time he was as soft as butter in the sun and scared stiff to show his true feelings.

Come to think of it, that real-life story might help explain the Enniscorthy poltergeist. John Randall was, by all accounts, a quiet, pleasant, likeable lad of eighteen. And his report of the haunting shows him to be intelligent, thoughtful, touched with a sense of humour. The kind of young man, in fact, that would attract a shy, perhaps rather retiring girl. And there was just such a young woman at 8 Court Street, someone so neglected by the rest of the household that she is hardly mentioned in the reports: Bridget Thorpe, the servant girl.

The Redmonds were not wealthy. Indeed, Mr Redmond was a labourer and his wife took in boarders to swell their earnings. The servant couldn't have been paid much (if anything). We can make a fairly informed guess that she was a skivvy – a badly off, almost destitute girl, slaving for the Redmonds in order to keep a roof over her head and food in her belly. Before 1914, the worst jobs in Britain's homes were done by such sad and often misused menials. Their only hope of rescue was marriage to a kindly husband.

So there at 8 Court Street is poor Bridget, eking out a miserable existence, when along come three boys to dazzle her eyes; and John Randall was, for her, the pick of the bunch. While the boys enjoyed each other's friendship and the satisfaction of their jobs, Bridget slaved in the kitchen, made their beds, heard them laughing and talking, and, no doubt, watched them longingly. She slept in the room above theirs, and it doesn't take much imagination to picture her lying in her lonely bed during those first few days of John's stay in the house and thinking of him sleeping just below her – dreaming of him as well, perhaps.

At any rate, I'm supposing that all Bridget's pent-up worries, her frustrations, her miseries, her loneliness were concentrated on those three young men, and on John in particular. And these deep, unconscious longings transmitted themselves into strange energies that pulled the bedclothes off John as he lay in bed, and generally gave all three lads a rough time – quite like the stone-throwing, shy boy I mentioned earlier. But, sad for Bridget, everyone's attention was focused on the result of the upset, not on the cause: they came to talk to John, and they watched as he was thrown about the room. No one said much to Bridget, or asked her what she thought. Even when the spotlight of interest shone at its brightest on the little house in Court Street, its beam hardly touched on poor Bridget. Until, in the end, her longings undiscovered by the only person that mattered to her, John himself, the household broke up and Bridget and John went their different ways. When, as was to be expected, the haunting ceased. For what hope now had Bridget of winning the attentions of her ideal mate?

I have to admit again that all this is guesswork. And until

there is more scientific knowledge to provide a sound solution based on properly conducted experiments, my ideas can be nothing better than a theory. But it is a theory that fits the known facts far more snugly — in my opinion, at least — than belief in witches as the cause of poltergeists, or in bogles, or in mischievous ghosts come back from the other side of death to annoy us. As for you, you must discover your own theory, and make up your mind about these puzzling phenomena.

PART FOUR

Ghost hunting

12 · Investigating Hauntings

By Renée Haynes

Stories about haunted places are always fascinating. What goes on there, and how, and why? If you like playing detective, you may want to know ways of finding out the answers to these questions.

Some hauntings can be explained as the results of ordinary trickery. In others some natural cause is at work, though it has not yet been traced. Both these possibilities can be tested.

Before going into details, though, two things need to be said. The first is that scientific methods of investigation can only show whether or not some physical cause is involved. The second is that if no physical cause can be found this does not mean that what is said to happen is 'simply imaginary', unreal, even mad. It does probably mean though that you are unlikely to see anything if you deliberately go and look for it. Remember the comic dialogue that Shakespeare wrote, making one character boast, 'I can call spirits from the vasty deep!' and another answer, 'Why so can I, and so can any man – But will they come when you do call for them?'

We do not know whether 'spirits' are always – or often – involved in hauntings. But we do know that whatever it is that takes place seems to occur quite unexpectedly, when people are relaxed, or thinking about something quite different.

Keeping your eyes and wits about you, making observations, writing them down and thinking them over: these are useful in detecting trickery, and the reasons why tricks are played. Dress-

129

ing up in a white sheet and jumping out from behind a wall at dusk with a scream sometimes appeals to the stupid and inconsiderate. Making a sensation, and enjoying the publicity, thrills others. Then there are those with something to hide. Smugglers used to spread rumours that the places where they landed their cargoes were haunted. This made local people keep away, and accounted for strange lights seen flitting about after dark, or peculiar sounds. Today just occasionally tenants who want to be moved from one house to another have been known to stage a 'haunt'.

There are many ordinary happenings which have frightened or startled people into believing they were caused by ghostly means. Subterranean movements of earth and rock in old mineworkings, for instance, can cause very odd noises, and miners hearing tappings and rumblings in the underground darkness used to be sure they were made either by earth spirits or by the spirits of other miners long dead. For centuries the luminous patches made by marsh gas rising from swamps were called Will o' the wisps, or Jack o' lanterns, and thought to be mischievous fairies who wanted to lure travellers into the mud. Only a hundred years ago French peasants spoke of certain fields as 'accursed' because the animals put to graze there fell ill and died. (The great French scientist Louis Pasteur found that the soil was infected with the germs of a terrible disease, anthrax.) In each of these cases, the facts were there all right, but the explanations were wrong.

Nowadays some very good ghost stories can be traced back to the shrieking of vixens on spring nights in the country, to the tapping caused by death-watch beetles in old timber, and to the snoring of young owls (their musical hootings, though eerie, are easier to recognize).

Alarming sounds, cold feelings, and even some apparitions can come from disturbances underground, far below the foundations of a house or garden. There are very few earthquakes in Britain, but there are sometimes tremors, especially round what are called geological faults, deep rifts in a stretch of rock. Here, as in those abandoned mine workings, subterranean movements can cause mysterious knockings and even noises like footsteps as they shake the whole structure of the house above. Long ago, houses used to be built with rows of bells in the basement. If you ever go to Blenheim Palace, have a look at them there. Each was rung by pulling a cord in one of the upstairs rooms, and over each bell was the name of its own particular room. Someone in the big basement hall, hearing a jingle, would come into the passage, see which bell was still vibrating, and then go upstairs to find out what was wanted: coal for the fire perhaps, as there was no gas, no electricity and no central heating. This system of bells was used in many buildings much smaller than Blenheim Palace. Most Victorian town houses had them. If, as sometimes happened, earth movements jangled them, people often jumped to the frightening conclusion that the bells were being rung by invisible hands.

These movements underground can also be caused by water. After heavy rain tiny streams bricked over long ago, and ancient drains, can fill up and press heavily on the surrounding soil. In old times, too, sewers were often made to run out into a river or estuary, and though they are no longer used, the pipes are often still there. When the river is full, or at especially high tides, water is forced up into those pipes again, they shake and creak, and the buildings above shake and creak with them. Sometimes mist comes up, and it is not difficult to mistake a column of white mist drifting along in the twilight for a ghost. Once when I was staying in my grandmother's house on the edge of a hill I ran out early one morning on to the lawn and saw little white clouds floating about the damp orchard below. In clear September sunshine there was no mistaking what they were. But if I

131

had bẹen walking up the steep orchard path alone in the evening at the time called 'between dog and wolf' I might have had other ideas.

For trying to find out whether physical causes are producing what looks like a haunt, you need first of all to get together a small team of fairly calm, sensible people. Six to eight is a good number. Then, armed with electric torches and one or two tape-recorders you can watch what if anything goes on in the various rooms of a 'haunted' house, and meet and compare notes from time to time.

Before beginning, you should look at the walls, inside and out, to see if there are cracks brought about by a subsidence, or any other movement that shakes the foundations. A geological map of the district should show whether there is any rift in the rock foundations beneath the house. It would also be useful, if you can manage it, to get hold of plans of sewers, underground streams, or old mine workings. These need not have anything to do with coal. They exist, for instance, under the disused tin mines of Cornwall. A camera that can take both ordinary and infra-red film is invaluable. If it will only take the ordinary sort then a flashlight attachment and a trip wire will make it possible to photograph automatically anyone playing tricks in the dark. Thermometers will show whether there are any physical changes in temperature. Powder scattered round objects – chairs, tables, vases, saucepans – that are said to move will show whether they have in fact done so, and also whether any marks have been made by someone moving them in the ordinary way. A tape measure will show exactly how far, if at all, movement has gone. If the 'haunting' only happens occasionally, say in spring and autumn, it will be worth checking whether there have been any very high tides during the previous twenty-four hours. This is, of course, for places not too far distant from the coast, or from tidal waters. In all cases it is worth while to look up recent rain-fall records. A heavy storm may have flooded the street drains or swelled forgotten streams.

As I said at the beginning, all that this kind of detective work can do is, of course, to find out whether there are recognizable 'natural causes' for what goes on in the 'haunt' you are investigating. There may be others that we simply do not understand.

Thus, a scientist I know was working one evening in a long room with a door at each end. He had a tape recorder switched on so he could speak into it any notes he wished to make. He thought everyone else in his department had gone home until he 'heard' one of the doors open and someone come walking along. He said something like 'Hallo, you're working late too, are you?' but there was no answer. When he looked up he could see no one, but he could still 'hear' the footsteps walking along and out at the other door. Mystified, he played back the tape recorder. No footsteps were audible, but his own voice was quite plain, saying 'Hallo, you're working late too, are you?' Obviously there was no physical cause for the other sounds or they would have emerged on the tape, which can be far more sensitive than human hearing. He had heard with his mind, not his ears.

This curious occurrence is typical of many 'hauntings'. It appears trivial and meaningless, and it shows how a sane, healthy person can feel sure he has 'heard' (or 'seen' or even 'smelled') something that is not physically there. Luckily this particular observer at once wrote down what had happened. Unless this is done, the tidying-up part of the mind that likes to find an explanation for everything sometimes gets to work to invent one. Then you get a good story that may not fit the facts.

So, if anything odd happens to you write it down as soon as possible, with the place, time, and date, sign it and get someone else to read it through and to write his or her name and address at the bottom as a witness. The record may be useful. The Society for Psychical Research would always like to see such records. Here is the kind of thing:

On Friday 11 August 1972, about 3 p.m., I went into the large south front room on the ground floor of 14 Hollyhock Square, Nelsonstown. It was a bright sunny afternoon. With his back to the mantelpiece lounged a young man with fair hair, a pink shirt and blue denim trousers. He straightened himself up, held out his hand to me and vanished.

Signed: John Smith, builder and decorator.
16 Dolphin Road, Nelsonstown, 11/viii/72

Witnessed: M. E. Leicester, housekeeper.
14 Hollyhock Square, Nelsonstown.
11 August 1972.

Mr Smith came straight to my room and told me what had happened. He then wrote it down. I guarantee that this is exactly what he told me. He was rather upset, and I made him a cup of tea. He caught sight of a framed photograph on a chest of drawers, and said, startled, 'That's the man I saw.' The photograph was of Denis Scott, who used to lodge here but died very suddenly three weeks ago.

Signed: M. E. Leicester.

If you are alone, and cannot get a team together to make technical observations and to watch, there is another way in which you can work. This means looking into the stories concerned with traditional hauntings, stories which become well known and make it easy for people to misinterpret what they see.

This kind of research will not necessarily explain how the stories began, but it may show whether they can possibly be true. For instance, there is a popular tale that Nell Gwynne, the seventeenth-century actress, haunts the Gargoyle Club on the fourth floor of a Georgian building in Soho. A careful examination of historical records has shown that this is most unlikely, as the house was not even built until seventy years after her death. The site had previously been used for stables, which were certainly not four storeys high.

For checking up on traditional tales you will find your local library enormously useful. You can read reminiscences and memoirs written about the time when the original incident is said to have happened. You can consult old street maps and look at contemporary documents. Many small ancient towns have fascinating records of the past. The little museum at Lyme Regis, for instance, owns many pages of the evidence given at a witch trial hundreds of years ago. There are also discoveries to be made in the great County Histories. One I know contains a lively report of a long poltergeist outbreak in Cromwell's time, then attributed to 'The Just Devil of Woodstock'.

Here again, as with the use of technical tests, you can often find out what a haunting is *not*, but not what it is.

How does it happen, for instance, that people see a ghost who have never heard that a place is said to be haunted? This occurred to a small boy I knew who saw a very tall woman in 'funny' clothes climbing a flight of stone steps in front of him, his elder sister, and their teacher. At the landing she turned and walked out of sight through a bricked-up door. The sisters and the teacher, who did not see her, were frightened – the boy was not – especially when they later discovered that the ghost of Edward VI's tall nurse was supposed to haunt that staircase. Four hundred years ago there had been a real door there, and she had passed through it.

There are a number of historical hauntings of this kind, where figures are 'seen' going through doors that no longer exist, or gliding along knee-deep in a new floor two feet above the level of the one they walked on in their day. It seems as if some kind of film were being shown over and over again. And in a film, of course, the real live actors are not there – only their pictures, and the sounds of their voices.

If we accept the possibility that some genuine traditional hauntings may have much in common with films, then there are two more questions to be answered. (There are always new questions in this kind of research.) The first is, how did they get recorded? The second is, why does not everyone see them?

No one knows for certain. It is possible to hazard a guess that such recordings may have happened when the people involved were feeling some intense emotional stress: fear, or fury, or worry, or despair. We do know, for instance, that Edward VI's nurse was terribly anxious about her own baby, which she had had to leave behind when she joined the royal household. Happy feelings, love and joy and wonder and peace, do not seem to set hauntings going, though I think they may become part of the 'atmosphere' of certain places.

As to why some people see these things and some do not, again we can only hazard an explanation. Research carried out by careful observation and by careful experiments in Britain, America, and other countries for nearly a hundred years now indicates that something called the psi factor, or extra-sensory perception (E.S.P. for short) may be at work (see Plate 9).

This varies a great deal between one person and another. Just as some people are musical geniuses, some are average, and some are tone deaf, so people are good, bad, or indifferent at E.S.P. Even people who are good at it cannot turn it on and off at will. Occasionally they will get a flash of sudden information about what is happening beyond the range of their senses. But they do not always understand what the information means, because it is all mixed up with their own ideas and thoughts. They do not always realize where it comes from, either.

Thus mediums, who are usually especially good at E.S.P., often think that all the information they get *must* come from the souls of the dead; whereas they may be receiving it from the minds of those who consult them, or from flashes of the past or even of the future.

There is on record a case in which a medium told a man that a friend of his was dead, and then described in vivid detail the house in a certain town where that friend had lived for a while. The man later went to the town, traced the house, and – found his friend very much alive. The curious thing was that he had not moved in until *after* the sitting with the medium.

Here we return to the sort of thing that happened with the tappings in old mine workings, the lights wandering over the marshes, the 'accursed' fields. The facts were accurately observed but the interpretations were wrong.

E.S.P. OR PSI

E.S.P. stands for 'extra-sensory perception' and means 'gaining information without the use of the five senses'. This is now properly called psi, *but there are many other names people give the faculty: they say they have a 'hunch', or 'make an inspired guess', or have 'second sight' or 'intuition'. The knowledge seems to come into your head 'out of the blue', or you feel something so strongly that you cannot resist acting on the feeling. Sometimes extra-sensory information comes into the mind as a vivid picture seen in the mind's eye like a film or photograph. And the information can have to do with events happening now, or which are to happen in the future or have happened in the past. E.S.P. jumps the barriers of time and space....*

Ghost hunting

So trying to use E.S.P. – if you think you have any – to investigate hauntings is unlikely to reveal the exact truth. If you believe some real, conscious person who is dead is involved, pray for that person's peace of mind.

13 · The S.P.R.

You cannot go far in a study of ghosts without coming across the S.P.R. – the Society for Psychical Research. Founded in 1882 by of group of scientists and scholars, it is the most reliable and useful of the organizations which inquire into psychic phenomena. Over the years, its members have collected for its archives a vast quantity of investigators' reports, descriptions of paranormal experiences, and the results of experiments. Its library contains all the important records and pamphlets on the subject. And its quarterly *Journal*, edited by Renée Haynes, who wrote Chapter 12 of this book, publishes information and articles about everything from accounts of haunted houses to the mathematical statistics relating to an inquiry into E.S.P. (extra-sensory perception).

The members of the S.P.R. do not necessarily agree about what they think ghosts are. Indeed, they do not necessarily agree that there are any such phenomena at all. They belong to the Society in order to share their views, to pool their resources and knowledge, and to encourage the proper, scientific study of a subject tangled with superstition, hearsay evidence and unthinking fears.

The headquarters of the S.P.R. is at 1 Adam and Eve Mews, Kensington, London W8 6UQ. There the archives, library and offices are housed. Membership can begin at 18 years of age, and though non-members genuinely interested in the Society's work are welcome, it is best to contact the Secretary beforehand to arrange a convenient time for a visit.

In the same way, the Secretary will always try and help people who have serious questions to ask or problems to do with psychical phenomena, but these should first be put into a letter, and a stamped addressed envelope should be included for a reply.

14 · A Ghost Guide

Here is a list of a few of the thousands of haunted places in Britain and Ireland, the most haunted countries in the world. No one can guarantee that, if you visit these or any other ghost-ridden spot, you will witness a haunting. Ghosts do not perform, as actors do, according to public demand and at set times announced in the newspapers. They come and go as they please and show themselves only to people with psychic gifts. Because this is so, I have tried to select, in the main, places worth visiting for other reasons than spectral ones only: for their history, perhaps, or their architectural interest, or the beauty of their surroundings. And if you set off on a ghost tour, it is as well to check beforehand that you will be allowed into the buildings mentioned and the times when you will be welcome.

The sentence or two about each place is meant as an appetizer. I hope you will want to follow up for yourself the hauntings that specially attract you, finding out more about them from books and records and original documents. This kind of research best begins, like charity, at home, discovering the ghosts and hauntings that belong to your neighbourhood. Every village in Britain, however small, is rich with legends and folk tales and stories old and new, making up a collection of psychic fact and fiction special to that area. As for the whole country, half a dozen books would not be enough for a complete account of all Britain's haunted sites. My list is just a sample for you to begin with.

BARBRECK, LOCH CRAIGNISH, ARGYLLSHIRE. A 'hooded maiden' haunts the estate; she is seen sitting on a rock but disappears if anyone approaches.

THE RECTORY, BARNACK, NORTHAMPTONSHIRE. A poltergeist upset Charles Kingsley, author of *The Water Babies*, when he lived here as a boy. The ghost is called 'Button Cap' because it is said to be the phantom of a former rector who wore a night cap with a button on it.

GARRICK'S HEAD HOTEL, BATH. An old inn where many disturbances have been reported: a poltergeist once threw the cash register off the bar counter; spectral figures have been seen in various parts of the house; a *Western Daily Press* journalist, among others, heard mysterious noises in the sitting room. The inn used to connect by a secret passage with the Theatre Royal next door, where ghosts have also been encountered.

BLICKLING HALL, NEAR AYLSHAM, NORFOLK. Once a year on the anniversary of Anne Boleyn's death – 19 May 1536 – a ghostly coach pulled by headless horses and driven by a headless coachman drives Anne, her own severed head resting on her knees, towards the hall, where the entire grisly apparition vanishes. Anne's father, Sir Thomas, also haunts the hall, sometimes accompanied by his daughter.

BORLEY RECTORY, NEAR LONG MELFORD, SUFFOLK. Once reputed to be the most haunted house in England, investigations were conducted there by all kinds of psychic experts (and some who weren't) during the 1930s. Mysteriously gutted by fire in 1939, an occurrence blamed on the resident poltergeist.

BRECKLES HALL, NEAR ATTLEBOROUGH, NORFOLK. A ghostly coach and horses is supposed to drive up to the hall at night, and out of it steps a breathtakingly lovely woman. If she looks at you, you die! A genuine priest's hole exists inside this Elizabethan brick mansion.

BREDE PLACE, STUBBS LANE, NEAR RYE, SUSSEX. A house with eerie rooms inhabited by at least one apparition – that of 'Father John', a priest who lived at Brede hundreds of years ago.

BUCKHOLM TOWER, NEAR GALASHIELS, SELKIRKSHIRE. A ruin said to be haunted every June by one of the Lairds of Buckholm, called Pringle, who, during his life, mistreated his people.

BURTON AGNES HALL, BURTON AGNES, NEAR DRIFFIELD, YORKSHIRE. See page 18.

THE CATHEDRAL, CANTERBURY, KENT. Accredited with a number of ghosts, among them being the spectre of Archbishop Simon Sudbury, murdered in 1381, which walks in the tower.

ST ANNE'S, PITTVILLE CIRCUS ROAD, CHELTENHAM, GLOUCESTERSHIRE. House where the famous 'Morton' ghost appeared, described in Chapter 6.

RENVYLE HOUSE, CONNEMARA, IRELAND. The ghost of a man who strangled himself has been seen in the house. The poet W. B. Yeats was one person who claimed to have met it.

PLAS MAWR HOUSE, CONWAY, CAERN. The old Lantern Room is thought to be haunted.

COOKSTOWN, COUNTY TYRONE, NORTHERN IRELAND. In a modern council house footsteps were heard on many occasions walking back and forth in one of the rooms. The apparition of a man was seen outside the house by neighbours.

CORTACHY CASTLE, ANGUS. A spectral drummer sounds his drum as a warning of the approaching death of any member of the Ogilvie family, who own the castle, no matter where they might be at the time.

CRATHES CASTLE, KINCARDINESHIRE. The Green Lady's room is haunted by the figure of a woman who walks to the fire-place and lifts a ghostly baby from the hearth. A few years ago the bones of a woman and child were found buried under the fireplace.

BLUE LION INN, CWM, NEAR RHYL, FLINTSHIRE. A farm labourer, John Henry, murdered in 1646, is supposed to haunt the inn. He has been seen by the landlord, and visitors have heard footsteps walking about in empty rooms.

THE VICARAGE, DEDDINGTON, OXFORDSHIRE. The Reverend Maurice Frost died here in 1962 and his ghost is said to have haunted the place since.

LYME PARK, DISLEY, CHESHIRE. A 'lady in white' – and her funeral procession – haunts the house and grounds. A skeleton was discovered in a small secret chamber beneath 'the ghost room'.

CLOUDS HILL, NEAR DORCHESTER, DORSET. T. E. Lawrence, the famous Lawrence of Arabia, died in 1935 driving his motor-cycle near his small cottage home, Clouds Hill. Since then re-peated reports have been made about apparitions seen entering the house and riding a spectral motorcycle near the spot where he died.

EDGEHILL, WARWICKSHIRE. Scene of a Civil War battle fought in 1642. The noise of battle has since been heard many times, and ghostly soldiers carrying flags, drums and firing guns have been seen. This famous haunting is described from tradi-tional records in *Ghosts* by William Mayne.

THE VICARAGE, ELM, NEAR WISBECH, CAMBRIDGESHIRE.

This two-hundred-year-old house is supposed to be haunted by a monk called Ignatius who died nearly 800 years ago burdened with guilt. He slept while on watch for floods rising from the fens. The floods came and drowned some of his brethren.

8 COURT STREET, ENNISCORTHY, COUNTY WEXFORD, IRELAND. Scene of the famous poltergeist haunting described in Chapter 11.

THE PARSONAGE, EPWORTH, ISLE OF AXHOLME, LINCOLNSHIRE. Birthplace of John Wesley, founder of Methodism, the parsonage suffered a poltergeist disturbance in 1716–17 involving many of the Wesley family, which was large. John later wrote an article about the haunting.

FARINGDON, BERKSHIRE. In 1963 and 1964 at Oriel Cottage on the Wicklesham Road the Wheeler family were so frightened by ghostly events that they called in the police, who agreed that there were 'strange noises' in the house. Twenty-one people saw a mysterious shape and felt cold draughts round their feet for which there was no explanation. The ghost was thought to belong to a lodger who had committed suicide in the cottage before the Wheelers came to live there.

THE PARISH CHURCH, FARNHAM, SURREY. A number of ghosts are said to inhabit the church: priests saying mass, processing figures with torches, and a little old lady.

FELBRIGGE HALL, NEAR NORWICH, NORFOLK. Haunted by one of the Windham family – and perhaps now by a Miss Kitton too. She told Augustus Hare: 'Mr Windham comes every night to look after his favourite books in the library. He goes straight to the shelves where they are: we hear him moving the tables and chairs about. We never disturb him though, for we intend to be ghosts ourselves some day.'

THE FORD AT FULMER, BUCKINGHAMSHIRE. The sound of an unseen horse and trap are sometimes heard here.

FYVIE CASTLE, ABERDEENSHIRE. A skeleton was found in a secret chamber, after which ghostly occurrences took place, including the apparition of a 'green lady'. The skeleton has been walled up again.

BRONTË STREET, GATESHEAD, COUNTY DURHAM. Poltergeists drove the Coulthard family out of the council house after a haunting in 1963 and 1964 during which furniture, crockery and ornaments were thrown about and broken.

GLAMIS CASTLE, ANGUS. The place where Macbeth murdered King Duncan and where the present Princess Margaret was born. The haunted room is the subject of many legends and stories.

THE OLD VICARAGE, GRANTCHESTER, CAMBRIDGESHIRE. Made famous by the poet Rupert Brooke, the house and an almost ruined building in the garden are said to be troubled by poltergeists.

ST ANNE'S CASTLE INN, GREAT LEIGHS, ESSEX. No one, it is said, sleeps undisturbed in the haunted room of what claims to be England's oldest inn. Those who try are woken by a variety of terrifying noises.

NATIONAL MARITIME MUSEUM, GREENWICH. A 'ghost' photograph was taken here in 1966. Subsequently, unexplained noises were heard by a party of ghost-hunters.

HAM HOUSE, RICHMOND, SURREY. A 'stately home' haunted by the Duchess of Lauderdale, who lived here during Cromwell's and King Charles II's days.

PENN PLACE, HAMPTON, MIDDLESEX. A 'grey lady', thought to be the ghost of Mrs Penn who nursed King Edward VI when he was a child, was seen many times by the small daughter of an artist, Eric Fraser, while living in the house.

HAMPTON COURT, MIDDLESEX. Mrs Penn (see above) also haunts here, along with a host of other spectres: Jane Seymour (King Henry VIII's third unfortunate wife), a phantom child, a white lady, Archbishop Laud, Lady Catherine Howard (whose apparition in the Haunted Gallery – see Plate 3 – re-enacts her ugly death), and, of course, England's busiest ghost – Anne Boleyn.

THE CASTLE, HASTINGS, SUSSEX. Thomas à Becket's ghost is said to haunt the castle – but only on autumn evenings!

BLACK HOUSE, HIGHER BRIXHAM, DEVONSHIRE. A monk is supposed to haunt this large old house, and has locked the owner in the bathroom, from which she had to be rescued by a carpenter who sawed through the locks and bolts.

HINTON AMPNER, NEAR ALRESFORD, HAMPSHIRE. One of Britain's most famous hauntings, an original 1772 account is reprinted in Harry Price's *Poltergeists Over England*, and a partly fictional version in William Mayne's *Ghosts*.

HINXWORTH PLACE, NEAR BALDOCK, HERTFORDSHIRE. Thuds, screams, the noise of a baby crying and of water coming from a pump in the yard are heard on stormy autumn evenings. Legend tells of the accidental killing of a child by its nurse many years ago.

FERRY BOAT INN ON THE RIVER OUSE AT HOLYWELL, HUNTINGDONSHIRE. The ghost of a young girl called Juliet rises from her burial place, now part of the floor of the bar of this inn, every year on 17 March, St Patrick's Day, the anniversary of the love-sick girl's suicide many hundreds of years ago. Unfortunately, as the bar is usually crowded on that night, Juliet rarely puts in an appearance these days.

4 EDEN STREET, HORDEN, COUNTY DURHAM. 'Ghostly presences' finally drove a miner and his wife from this house in 1967 after the local vicar had tried unsuccessfully to exorcise the phenomena.

THE ROYAL HOTEL, HOYLAKE, CHESHIRE. The figure of a man dressed in tweeds and a cap puts in an appearance now and again.

HERSTMONCEUX CASTLE, NEAR EASTBOURNE, SUSSEX. Now the Royal Observatory, a number of ghost stories are told about this place, including one about a White Lady who was seen swimming in the moat.

BOSWORTH HALL, HUSBAND'S BOSWORTH, LEICESTER-SHIRE. Groans and creakings, the apparition of a former mistress of the house, Lady Lisgar, and a three-hundred-year-old bloodstain that's always damp haunt this historic building.

KILKENNY, IRELAND. The spectre of a tall, thin woman with flowing white hair and walking with the aid of crutches was seen in May 1969 near St John's parochial hall.

LEIGHTON BUZZARD, BEDFORDSHIRE. At Sid Mularney's motorcycle workshop in 1963 a poltergeist hurled spanners and other objects around the room while Sid was working, and disturbed neighbours with its 'strange bangings and clatterings'. See page 96.

SPEDLIN'S TOWER, LOCKERBIE, DUMFRIESSHIRE. A phantom, said to be the ghost of a miller murdered in the late seventeenth century, haunts this place.

LONDON GHOSTS:
Amen Court near St Paul's Cathedral. A 'shape' crawls along the top of a wall at night, its scraping boots and a rattling chain being heard as it does so.

The Bank of England, Threadneedle Street. The figure of an old lady appears in the Bank's garden, once a churchyard.

50 Berkeley Square. Once haunted by a terrifying apparition of no recognizable shape. London's best-known ghost and the source of what is in my opinion the best fictional ghost story ever written, *The Haunted and the Haunters* by Edward Bulwer-Lytton.

Birdcage Walk, St James's Park. A headless woman walking from Cockpit Steps to the lake has been seen by soldiers billeted in nearby Wellington Barracks, itself possessed of a ghost or two.

The Theatre Royal, Drury Lane. During matinées a 'man in grey' has been seeen many times sitting in the upper circle; a dressing room is haunted by the great comedian, Dan Leno.

St Dunstan's Church, East Acton. Ghostly figures process up the aisle.

The Church of St Magnus the Martyr, by London Bridge. A robed figure, often observed during the daylight hours, haunts here.

The Tower of London. Most haunted place in the capital, which isn't surprising after all the executions, tortures and other inhumanities history has concentrated into this fortress since William I built it. Among others are: the Countess of Salisbury, re-enacting her death, one of the ugliest ever witnessed; Sir Walter Raleigh; and, once again, Anne Boleyn, sometimes wearing her head and sometimes without.

THE CASTLE, LUDLOW, SHROPSHIRE. An apparitional white lady and the sound of heavy breathing haunt this eleventh-century building.

BISHAM ABBEY, NEAR MARLOW, BUCKINGHAMSHIRE. Now

a physical training centre, this old house was the scene of a bizarre event and a strange haunting. See page 16.

BETTISCOMBE MANOR, MARSHWOOD VALE, DORSET. Home of another of the 'screaming' skulls, like that at Burton Agnes Hall. It is kept in the house and causes dire troubles if removed. Origin unknown, but many legends are attached to it.

MEGGERNIE CASTLE, PERTHSHIRE. Haunted by the upper half of a female figure.

THE QUEEN'S HOTEL, MONMOUTH, MONMOUTHSHIRE. An attempt was made on Oliver Cromwell's life in one of the bedrooms (which still has bullet holes in the rafters) and a ghost is said to appear in shadowy form.

NEWTON-LE-WILLOWS, LANCASHIRE. Marching feet are supposed to be heard during August, in which month during 1648 a Highland battalion was found there by Cromwell's soldiers, who hanged the Scotsmen from the trees.

WILLINGTON QUAY, NORTH SHIELDS, NORTHUMBERLAND. The old mill was the site of a famous poltergeist haunting more than a hundred years ago.

PEEL CASTLE, ISLE OF MAN. Haunted by a ghostly dog.

FOUNTAINHALL HOUSE (SOMETIMES CALLED PENKAET CASTLE), PENCAITLAND, EAST LOTHIAN. Figures identified as belonging to King Charles I, a murdered owner, John Cockburn, and a hanged beggar, Alexander Hamilton, make appearances from time to time.

THE DOLPHIN INN, PENZANCE, CORNWALL. Possesses a spectral sea captain complete with lace collar and cuffs and a three-cornered hat.

PRESTBURY, NEAR CHELTENHAM, GLOUCESTERSHIRE. A

village teeming with ghosts! The Black Abbot appears at least three times a year in different spots. The ghost of Cleve Corner house is said to strangle anyone who sleeps in the haunted room. A cavalier gallops through Burgage and Mill lanes. Old Moses, a race-horse trainer, appears in Walnut Cottage. And a young girl is to be encountered now and then playing a spinet in the garden of Sundial Cottage.

RAYNHAM HALL, NEAR FAKENHAM, NORFOLK. The figure of the unhappy Dorothy Townshend, known as the Brown Lady, appears now and again, especially on the fine oak staircase where it was photographed. See page 74.

RINGCROFT, GALLOWAY. Scene of a famous poltergeist haunting in which a farmer called Andrew Mackie and his family were pulled from their beds by invisible hands, had stones thrown at them even inside the house, and were in other ways mistreated.

SAMLESBURY OLD HALL, NEAR BLACKBURN, LANCASHIRE. Phantom lovers – a lady in white and a man slain by her brother – still meet in the grounds.

THE BEACH AT SANDWOOD BAY, CAPE WRATH, SUTHERLAND. A bearded sailor wearing sea-boots and a weathered seaman's coat with brass buttons appears here and at the ruined Sandwood cottage, where frightening noises have been heard.

DANEWAY HOUSE, SAPPERTON, NEAR CIRENCESTER, GLOUCESTERSHIRE. Three ghosts live here: a girl who shakes a duster from a top-floor window, a woman who sits in a high-backed chair in the sitting-room, and a man dressed in a jerkin and carrying wine from the cellar.

SEDGEMOOR, SOMERSET. The sound of battle can sometimes be heard, said to be the noise of ghostly soldiers re-enacting the 1685 Battle of Sedgemoor.

151

Ghost hunting

BALLECHIN HOUSE, STRATHRAY, NEAR DUNKELD, PERTH-SHIRE. Famous hauntings in the 1890s: rattling, knockings, loud bangings, groans, voices heard from locked and empty rooms. Nine apparitions were seen by ghost-hunters: a nun, the nun's friend, a limping man, a black dog, a priest, the upper half of an old woman, another woman holding a cross, a man who shuffled and seemed to be old, and the phantom of a man still alive at the time. This was one of the first hauntings ever to be investigated by psychical researchers, and they did not do a very skilled job. The case is still argued about.

JAROLEN HOUSE, RODBOROUGH, STROUD, GLOUCESTER-SHIRE. Persistent reports of a ghostly grey lady, friendly and in-quisitive, who is particularly interested in domestic matters like ironing.

THE RECTORY, SYDERSTONE, NORFOLK. Scene of a famous poltergeist haunting that lasted for over forty years, coming to a climax in 1833. The house is near the site of Syderstone Hall, now gone, the home of Amy Robsart, who married Robert Dud-ley, Earl of Leicester in Queen Elizabeth's reign. Amy's ghost is still supposed to haunt the area.

THE CASTLE, TAMWORTH, STAFFORDSHIRE. A Black Lady and a White Lady each haunts her own part of the castle. In a 'haunted room' are heard ghostly sighs and groans.

THE MANOR HOUSE, TIDWORTH, WILTSHIRE. In 1661 polter-geists haunted the house in what is now called the case of 'The Tedworth Drummer'.

WARDLEY HALL, LANCASHIRE. Another house with a 'scream-ing skull'.

WATERFORD, MUNSTER, IRELAND. A vampire is supposed to be buried in the tiny graveyard by the ruined church.

CORBY CASTLE, WETHERAL, CUMBERLAND. In the castle's haunted bedroom has been seen from time to time a bright flame-like light enveloping a 'radiant boy' dressed in white clothes and looking very beautiful. He is said to come as a warning of death.

WHITBY, YORKSHIRE. A bogle called Hob, so the local people say, causes cars to skid, turns signposts round in the wrong direction and generally upsets motorists using roads in the vicinity of the town.

WIDECOMBE-IN-THE-MOOR, DARTMOOR, DEVON. A hundred years ago Mary Jay hanged herself two miles north of the village. Fresh flowers appear on her unconsecrated grave and no one can explain how they get there. In 1967, seventeen-year-old Rosemary Long saw a figure crouched over the grave, which, she said, looked like a man covered with a blanket. But the apparition had no face, and though the blanket stopped a foot above the ground, there were no legs or feet to be seen. Others have reported seeing a similar phantom.

WINCHCOMBE, NEAR CHELTENHAM, GLOUCESTERSHIRE. A tall, hooded figure walks along the road – called 'The Monk's Walk' for obvious reasons – at night. The oddest thing of all is that the apparition walks two feet above the ground.

WINDSOR CASTLE, WINDSOR, BERKSHIRE. The ghosts of Henry VIII, Elizabeth I, Charles I, and George III are all said to appear, besides other ghosts.

ST MARY'S CHURCH, WOODFORD, NORTHAMPTONSHIRE. In 1966 a young man, Gordon Carroll, took an interesting 'ghost photograph' of a figure kneeling in front of the altar. See page 73.

HOLY TRINITY CHURCH, MICKLEGATE, YORK. Among this beautiful city's apparitions is one of a hooded woman, said to be an Abbess from pre-Reformation days, who appears here.

Book List

The following books are recommended to anyone wishing to go on from the sketchy beginnings I have offered.

ASHBY, Robert H., *A Guidebook for the Study of Psychical Research*, Rider/Hutchinson, 1972.

BARDENS, Dennis, *Ghosts and Hauntings*, The Zeus Press, 1965.

BENNETT, Sir Ernest, *Apparitions and Haunted Houses*, Faber and Faber, 1939.

BRIGGS, Katharine M., *A Dictionary of British Folk-tales*, 4 vols., Routledge & Kegan Paul, 1970 and 1971.

CARRINGTON, Hereward and FODOR, Nandor, *The Story of the Poltergeist down the Centuries*, Rider & Company, 1953.

EDMUNDS, Simeon, *'Spirit' Photography*, Society for Psychical Research, 1965.

JACOBS, Joseph, *English Fairy Tales*, The Bodley Head, 1968.

MACKENZIE, Andrew, *Apparitions and Ghosts*, Arthur Barker, 1971.

MAYNE, William, *Ghosts*, Hamish Hamilton, 1971.

RUSSELL, Eric, *Ghosts*, Batsford, 1970.

SITWELL, Sacheverell, *Poltergeists*, Faber and Faber, 1940.

TYRRELL, G. N. M., *Apparitions*, Gerald Duckworth and the S.P.R., rev. ed. 1953.

WEST, D. J., *Psychical Research Today*, Gerald Duckworth, 1954.

Some of the well-known ghost stories mentioned in the text I have told as stories in my books: *Haunted Houses* and *More Haunted Houses* (Pan-Piccolo, 1971 and 1973). Readers who would like to study E.S.P. should read *The Hidden Springs* by Renée Haynes (Hutchinson, new edition 1973).

Index

Index